Puffin Books

# The Great Gilly Hopkins

For Gilly Hopkins life had been one foster home after another. And if there was a single lesson she had learned, it was that you had to be tough to survive. It wasn't enough that she was super intelligent – she had to make herself super cool and super tough too.

But then came a spell with big, bible-bashing Maime Trotter – the most unlikely foster mother you could imagine. Except that slowly, in fits and starts, a change began to come over Gilly. So that when her real mother appears on the scene, things are not quite so simple as they might have been . . .

Gilly Hopkins is an unforgettable character. With her longing to find her true place in life, she is comic and pathetic, scandalous and sympathetic – and *very* appealing. Despite her special circumstances, many eleven- and twelve-year-olds will find much in her to identify with.

This book won the Children's National Book Award in the U.S.A.

Also available in Puffin is Katherine Paterson's *Bridge to Terabithia*.

# KATHERINE PATERSON
# The Great Gilly Hopkins

PUFFIN BOOKS

Puffin Books, Penguin Books Ltd, Harmondsworth, Middlesex, England
Penguin Books, 625 Madison Avenue, New York, New York 10022, U.S.A.
Penguin Books Australia Ltd, Ringwood, Victoria, Australia
Penguin Books Canada Ltd, 2801 John Street, Markham, Ontario, Canada
L3R 1B4
Penguin Books (N.Z.) Ltd, 182–190 Wairau Road, Auckland 10, New Zealand

First published in the United States of America by T.Y. Crowell and Co. 1978
First published in Great Britain by Victor Gollancz Ltd 1979
Published in Puffin Books 1981

Set in Baskerville
by Syarikat Seng Teik Sdn. Bhd., Kuala Lumpur, Malaysia.
Made and printed in Great Britain by
Cox & Wyman Ltd, Reading

*For Mary*
*from her real and adopted mother with love*

# Contents

# Welcome to Thompson Park

'Gilly,' said Miss Ellis with a shake of her long blond hair toward the passenger in the back seat. 'I need to feel that you are willing to make some effort.'

Galadriel Hopkins shifted her bubble gum to the front of her mouth and began to blow gently. She blew until she could barely see the shape of the social worker's head through the pink bubble.

'This will be your third home in less than three years.' Miss Ellis swept her golden head left to right and then began to turn the wheel in a cautious manoeuvre to the left. 'I would be the last person to say that it was all your fault. The Dixons' move to Florida, for example. Just one of those unfortunate things. And Mrs Richmond having to go into the hospital' – it seemed to Gilly that there was a long, thoughtful pause before the caseworker went on – 'for her nerves.'

*Pop!*

Miss Ellis flinched and glanced in the rear-view mirror but continued to talk in her calm, professional voice while Gilly picked at the bits of gum stuck in her straggly bangs and on her cheeks and chin. 'We should have been more alert to her condition before placing any foster child there. *I* should have been more alert.' Cripes, thought Gilly. The woman was getting sincere. What a pain. 'I'm not trying to *blame* you, Gilly. It's just that I need, we all need, your cooperation if any kind of arrangement is to work out.' Another pause. 'I can't imagine you *enjoy* all this moving around.' The blue eyes in the mirror were checking out Gilly's response. 'Now this new foster mother is very different from Mrs Nevins.' Gilly calmly pinched a blob of gum off the end of her nose. There was no use trying to get the gum out of her hair. She sat back and tried to chew the bit she had managed to salvage. It stuck to her teeth in a thin layer. She fished another ball of gum from her jeans pocket and scraped the lint off with her thumbnail before elaborately popping it into her mouth.

'Will you do me a favour, Gilly? Try to get off on the right foot?'

Gilly had a vision of herself sailing around the living room of the foster home on her right foot like an ice skater. With her uplifted left foot she was shoving the next foster mother square in the mouth. She smacked her new supply of gum in satisfaction.

'Do me another favour, will you? Get rid of that bubble gum before we get there?'

Gilly obligingly took the gum out of her mouth while Miss Ellis's eyes were still in the mirror. Then when the social worker turned her attention back to the traffic, Gilly carefully spread the gum under the handle of the left-hand door as a sticky surprise for the next person who might try to open it.

Two traffic lights farther on Miss Ellis handed back a towelette. 'Here,' she said, 'see what you can do about that guck on your face before we get there.'

Gilly swiped the little wet paper across her mouth and dropped it on the floor.

'Gilly –' Miss Ellis sighed and shifted her fancy on-the-floor gears. 'Gilly –'

'My name,' Gilly said between her teeth, 'is Galadriel.'

Miss Ellis appeared not to have heard. 'Gilly, give Maime Trotter half a chance, OK? She's really a nice person.'

That cans it, thought Gilly. At least nobody had accused Mr or Mrs Nevins, her most recent foster parents, of being 'nice'. Mrs Richmond, the one with the bad nerves, had been 'nice'. The Newman family, who couldn't keep a five-year-old who wet her bed, had been 'nice'. Well, I'm eleven now, folks, and, in case you haven't heard, I don't wet my bed anymore. But I am not nice. I am brilliant. I am famous across this entire country. Nobody wants to tangle with the great Galadriel Hopkins. I am too clever and too hard to manage. Gruesome Gilly, they call me. She leaned back comfortably. Here I come, Maime baby, ready or not.

They had reached a neighbourhood of huge trees and old houses. The social worker slowed and stopped beside a dirty white fence. The house it penned was old and brown with a porch that gave it a sort of potbelly.

Standing on the porch, before she rang the bell, Miss Ellis took out a comb. 'Would you try to pull this through your hair?'

Gilly shook her head. 'Can't.'

'Oh, come on, Gilly –'

'No. Can't comb my hair. I'm going for the Guinness Record for uncombed hair.'

'Gilly, for pete's sake . . .'

'Hey, there, I thought I heard y'all pull up.' The door had opened, and a huge hippopotamus of a woman was filling the doorway. 'Welcome to Thompson Park, Gilly, honey.'

'Galadriel,' muttered Gilly, not that she expected this bale of blubber to manage her real name. Jeez, they didn't have to put her in with a freak.

Half a small face, topped with muddy brown hair and masked with thick metal-rimmed glasses, jutted out from behind Mrs Trotter's mammoth hip.

The woman looked down. 'Well, 'scuse me, honey.' She

put her arm around the head as if to draw it forward, but the head resisted movement. 'You want to meet your new sister, don't you? Gilly, this is William Ernest Teague.'

The head immediately disappeared behind Mrs Trotter's bulk. She didn't seem bothered. 'Come in, come in. I don't mean to leave you standing on the porch like you was trying to sell me something. You belong here now.' She backed up. Gilly could feel Miss Ellis's fingers on her backbone gently prodding her through the doorway and into the house.

Inside, it was dark and crammed with junk. Everything seemed to need dusting.

'William Ernest, honey, you want to show Gilly where her room is?'

William Ernest clung to the back of Mrs Trotter's flowered housedress, shaking his head.

'Oh, well, we can see to that later.' She led them down the hallway to a living room. 'Just sit down and make yourself at home, now.' She smiled all across her face at Gilly, like the 'After' in a magazine diet ad – a 'Before' body with an 'After' smile.

The couch was brown and squat with a pile of cushions covered in greying lace at the far end. A matching brown chair with worn arms slumped at the opposite side of the room. Grey lace curtains hung at the single window between them, and beside the window was a black table supporting an old-time TV set with rabbit ears. The Nevinses had had colour TV. On the right-hand wall between the door and the brown chair stood a black upright piano with a dusty brown bench. Gilly took one of the pillows off the couch and used it to wipe every trace of dust off the piano bench before sitting down on it.

From the brown chair Miss Ellis was staring at her with a very nonprofessional glare. Mrs Trotter was lowering herself to the sofa and chuckling. 'Well, we been needing somebody to rearrange the dust around here. Ain't we, William Ernest, honey?'

William Ernest climbed up behind the huge woman and lay behind her back like a bolster pillow, poking his head around from time to time to sneak another look at Gilly.

She waited until Mrs Trotter and Miss Ellis were talking, then gave little W.E. the most fearful face in all her repertory of scary looks, sort of a cross between Count Dracula and Godzilla. The little muddy head disappeared faster than a toothpaste cap down a sink drain.

She giggled despite herself. Both of the women turned to look at her. She switched easily and immediately to her 'Who, me?' look.

Miss Ellis stood up. 'I need to be getting back to the office, Mrs Trotter. You'll let me know' – she turned to Gilly with prickles in her big blue eyes – 'you'll let me know if there're any problems?'

Gilly favoured Miss Ellis with her best barracuda smile.

Meantime Mrs Trotter was laboriously hefting herself to her feet. 'Don't worry, Miz Ellis. Gilly and William Ernest and me is nearly friends already. My Melvin, God rest him, used to say that Trotter never met a stranger. And if he'd said kid, he woulda been right. I never met a kid I couldn't make friends with.'

Gilly hadn't learned yet how to vomit at will, but if she had, she would have dearly loved to throw up on that one. So, lacking the truly perfect response, she lifted her legs and spun around to the piano, where she proceeded to bang out 'Heart and Soul' with her left hand and 'Chopsticks' with her right.

William Ernest scrambled off the couch after the two women, and Gilly was left alone with the dust, the out-of-tune piano, and the satisfaction that she had indeed started off on the right foot in her new foster home. She could stand anything, she thought – a gross guardian, a freaky kid, an ugly, dirty house – as long as she was in charge.

She was well on the way.

# The Man Who Comes
to Supper

The room that Mrs Trotter took Gilly to was about the
size of the Nevinses' new station wagon. The narrow bed
filled up most of the space, and even someone as skinny as
Gilly had to kneel on the bed in order to pull out the
drawers of the bureau opposite it. Mrs Trotter didn't even
try to come in, just stood in the doorway slightly swaying
and smiling, her breath short from climbing the stairs.

'Why don't you just put your things away in the bureau
and get yourself settled? Then when you feel like it, you
can come on down and watch TV with William Ernest, or
come talk to me while I'm fixing supper.'

What an awful smile she had, Gilly thought. She didn't
even have all her teeth. Gilly dropped her suitcase on the
bed and sat down beside it, kicking the bureau drawers
with her toes.

'You need anything, honey, just let Trotter know, OK?'

Gilly jerked her head in a nod. What she needed was to
be left alone. From the bowels of the house she could hear
the theme song from *Sesame Street*. Her first job would be to
improve W.E.'s taste in TV. That was for sure.

'It's goin' to be OK, honey. I know it's been hard to
switch around so much.'

'I like moving.' Gilly jerked one of the top drawers so
hard it nearly came out onto her head. 'It's boring to stay
in one place.'

'Yeah.' The big woman started to turn and then hesitated. 'Well –'

Gilly slid off the bed and put her left hand on the door-knob and stuck her right hand on her hip.

Mrs Trotter glanced down at the hand on the knob. 'Well, make yourself at home. You hear now?'

Gilly slammed the door after her. God! Listening to that woman was like licking melted ice cream off the carton. She tested the dust on the top of the bureau, and then, standing on the bed, wrote in huge cursive curlicues, 'Ms Galadriel Hopkins'. She stared at the lovely letters she had made for a moment before slapping down her open palm in the middle of them and rubbing them all away.

The Nevinses' house had been square and white and dustless, just like every other square, white, dustless house in the treeless development where they had lived. She had been the only thing in the neighbourhood out of place. Well, Hollywood Gardens was spotless once more. They'd got rid of her. No. She'd got rid of them – the whole stinking lot.

Unpacking even just the few things in her brown suitcase always seemed a waste of time to Gilly. She never knew if she'd be in a place long enough to make it worth the bother. And yet it was something to fill the time. There were two little drawers at the top and four larger ones below. She put her underwear in one of the little ones, and her shirts and jeans in one of the big ones, and then picked up the photograph from the bottom of the suitcase.

Out of the pasteboard frame and through the plastic cover the brown eyes of the woman laughed up at her was they always did. The glossy black hair hung in gentle waves without a hair astray. She looked as though she as the star of some TV show, but she wasn't. See – right there in the corner she had written 'For my beautiful Galadriel, I will always love you.' She wrote that to me, Gilly told herself, as she did each time she looked at it, only to me. She turned the frame over. It was still there – the little piece of tape with the name on it. 'Courtney Rutherford Hopkins.'

Gilly smoothed her own straw-coloured hair with one hand as she turned the picture over again. Even the teeth were gorgeous. Weren't girls supposed to look like their mothers? The word 'mother' triggered something deep in her stomach. She knew the danger signal. Abruptly she shoved the picture under a T-shirt and banged the bureau drawer shut. This was not the time to start dissolving like hot Jell-O. She went downstairs.

'There you are, honey.' Trotter turned away from the sink to greet her. 'How about giving me a hand here with this salad?'

'No.'

'Oh.'

Score a point for Gilly.

'Well' – Trotter shifted her weight to her left foot, keeping her eyes on the carrots she was scraping – 'William Ernest is in the living room watching *Sesame Street*.'

'My god, you must think I'm mental or something.'

'Mental?' Trotter moved to the kitchen table and started chopping the carrots on a tiny round board.

'Dumb, stupid.'

'Never crossed my mind.'

'Then why the hell you think I'm going to watch some retard show like that?'

'Listen here, Gilly Hopkins. One thing we better get straight right now tonight. I won't have you making fun of that boy.'

'I wasn't making fun of that boy.' What was the woman talking about? She hadn't mentioned the boy.

'Just 'cause someone isn't quite as smart as you are, don't give you no right to look down on them.'

'Who'm I looking down on?'

'You just said' – the fat woman's voice was rising, and her knife was crashing down on the carrots with vengeance – 'you just said William Ernest was' – her voice dropped to a whisper – 'retarded.'

'I did not. I don't even know the stupid kid. I never saw him in my life before today.'

Trotter's eyes were still flashing, but her hand and voice were under control. 'He's had a rough time of it in this world, but he's with Trotter now, and as long as the Lord leaves him in this house, ain't anybody on earth gonna hurt him. *In any way.*'

'Good god. All I was trying to say –'

'One more thing. In this house we don't take the Lord's name in vain.'

Gilly threw both her hands up in mock surrender. 'All right, all right. Forget it.' She started for the door.

'Supper's 'bout ready. How about going next door and getting Mr Randolph? He eats here nights.'

The word No was just about to pop out of Gilly's mouth, but one look at Trotter's eyes, and she decided to save her fights for something more important. 'Which house?'

'The grey one on the right.' She waved her knife vaguely uphill. 'Just knock on the door. If you do it good and loud, he'll hear you. Better take your jacket. Cold out.'

Gilly ignored the last. She ran out the door, through the picket gate, and onto the porch next door, stomping and jumping to keep warm. *Bam, bam, bam.* It was too cold for October. Mr Randolph's house was smaller and more grubby-looking even than Trotter's. She repeated her knock.

Suddenly the door swung inward, revealing a tiny shrunken man. Strange whitish eyes stared out of a wrinkled, brown face.

Gilly took one look and ran back to Trotter's kitchen as fast as she could go.

'What's the matter? Where's Mr Randolph?'

'I don't know. He's gone. He's not there.'

'What d'you mean he's not there?' Trotter began wiping her hands on her apron and walking toward the door.

'He's gone. Some weird little coloured man with white eyes came to the door.'

'Gilly! That was Mr Randolph. He can't see a thing. You've got to go back and bring him by the hand, so he won't fall.'

Gilly backed away. 'I never touched one of those people in my life.'

'Well, then, it's about time, ain't it?' Trotter snapped. 'Of course, if you can't manage, I can always send William Ernest.'

'I can manage. Don't you worry about me.'

'You probably got Mr Randolph all confused and upset by now.'

'Well, you shoulda warned me.'

'Warned *you*?' Trotter banged a spoon on the table. 'I shoulda warned poor Mr Randolph. You want me to send William Ernest?'

'I said I could manage. Good god!' At this, Trotter's spoon went up in the air like a fly-swatter. 'All right! I didn't say it. Hell, a person can't even talk around here.'

'A smart person like you oughta be able to think of a few regular words to stick in amongst the cusses.' The spoon went into the salad and stirred. 'Well, hurry up, if you're going.'

The little black man was still standing in the open doorway. 'William Ernest?' he called gently as Gilly started up the steps.

'No,' she said sharply. 'Me.'

'Oh.' He smiled widely although his eyes did not seem to move. 'You must be the new little girl.' He stretched out his right hand. 'Welcome to you, welcome.'

Gilly carefully took the elbow instead of the hand. 'Trotter said for me to get you for supper.'

'Well, thank you, thank you.' He reached behind, fumbling until he found the knob, and pulled the door shut. 'Kind of chilly tonight, isn't it?'

'Yeah.'

All she could think of was Miss Ellis. OK, so she hadn't been so great at the Nevinses', but she hadn't done anything to deserve this. A house run by a fat, fluff-brained religious fanatic with a mentally retarded seven-year-old – well, maybe he was and maybe he wasn't actually retarded, but chances were good the kid was running around with less than his full share of brains or why would Trotter make such a big deal of it? But she could've handled the two of them. It wasn't fair to throw in a blind black man who came to eat.

Or maybe Miss Ellis didn't know. Maybe Trotter kept this a secret.

The sidewalk was uneven. Mr Randolph's toe hit a high corner, and he lurched forward.

'Watch it!' Without thinking, Gilly threw her arms around the thin shoulders and caught him before he fell.

'Thank you, thank you.' Gilly dropped her arms. She thought for a horrible moment that he was going to try to grab her hand, but he didn't.

Boy, Miss Ellis, are you ever going to be sorry you did this to me.

'Now Mrs Trotter did tell me your name, but I'm ashamed to say I don't seem to recall it.' He tapped his head with its short, curly grey hair. 'I can keep all the luxuries up here, but none of the necessities.'

'Gilly,' she muttered.

'I beg your pardon?'

'Gilly Hopkins.'

'Oh, yes.' He was shuffling painfully up Trotter's front steps. Jeez. Why didn't he get a white cane or something? 'I am most pleased to make your acquaintance, Miss Gilly. I feel mighty close to all Mrs Trotter's children. Little William Ernest is like a grandson to me. So I feel sure...'

'Watch the door!'

'Yes, yes, I thank you.'

'Is that you, Mr Randolph?' came Trotter's voice from inside.

'Yes, indeed, Mrs Trotter, with the sweetest little escort you'd ever hope to see.'

Trotter appeared in the hallway with her hands on her hips. 'How you doing in this cold weather?'

'Not my best, I'm afraid. This sweet little girl had to keep me from falling right down on my face.'

'Did she now?'

See there, Trotter? I managed.

'I guess this old house is going to be a bit more lively now, eh, Mrs Trotter?'

'Wouldn't be surprised,' answered Trotter in a flat voice that Gilly couldn't read the meaning of.

The meal proceeded without incident. Gilly was hungry but thought it better not to seem to enjoy her supper too much. William Ernest ate silently and steadily with only an occasional glance at Gilly. She could tell that the child was scared silly of her. It was about the only thing in the last two hours that had given her any real satisfaction. Power over the boy was sure to be power over Trotter in the long run.

'I declare, Mrs Trotter,' said Mr Randolph, 'every day I think to myself, tonight's supper couldn't be as delicious as last night's. But I tell you, this is the most delicious meal I have ever had the privilege of eating.'

'Mr Randolph, you could flatter the stripe off a pole-cat.'

Mr Randolph let out a giggling laugh. 'It isn't flattery, I assure you, Mrs Trotter. William Ernest and Miss Gilly will bear me out in this. I may be old, but I haven't lost my sense of taste, even if some folks maintain I've lost the other four.'

They went on and on like that. Mr Randolph flattering the fat woman, and the fat woman eating it up like hot-fudge sundae with all the nuts.

What I should do, thought Gilly, as she lay that night in the narrow bed with her arms folded under her head, What I should do is write my mother. Courtney Ruther-ford Hopkins would probably sue county welfare if she knew what kind of place they'd forced her daughter to come to.

Miss Ellis (whose eyebrows always twitched when Gilly asked questions about Courtney) had once told her that Courtney was from Virginia. Everybody knew, didn't they, that families like Courtney's did not eat with coloured people? Courtney Rutherford Hopkins was sure to go into a rage, wasn't she, when she heard that news? Perhaps the self-righteous Trotter would be put into jail for contribut-ing to the delinquency of a minor. Miss Ellis would, of course, be fired. *Yum!*

She'll come to get me then, for sure, thought Gilly. Her mother wouldn't stand for her beautiful Galadriel to be in a dump like this for one single minute, once she knew. But how was she to know? Miss Ellis would never admit it. What kind of lies was the social worker telling Courtney to keep her from coming to fetch Gilly?

As she dropped off to sleep, Gilly promised herself for the millionth time that she would find out where Courtney Rutherford Hopkins was, write to her, and tell her to come and take her beautiful Galadriel home.

# More Unpleasant Surprises

In the tiny mirror over the bureau Gilly noted with no little satisfaction that her hair was a wreck. Yesterday before the bubble gum got into it, it had looked as though it simply needed combing. Today it looked like a lot that had been partially bulldozed – an uprooted tree here, a half wall with a crumbling chimney there. It was magnificent. It would run Trotter wild. Gilly bounced down the stairs and into the kitchen.

She held her head very straight as she sat at the kitchen table and waited for the fireworks.

'I'll take you down to the school a little after nine, hear?' Trotter said.

Of course Gilly heard. She tilted her head a little in case Trotter couldn't *see*.

'If I take you down earlier,' Trotter went on, 'we'll just have to sit and wait till they can take care of us. I'd as leave sit here at my own table with a cup of coffee, wouldn't you?' She put a bowl of steaming hot cereal down in front of Gilly.

Gilly nodded her head vigorously Yes.

William Ernest was staring at her, his glasses steamed up from the oatmeal. Gilly bared her teeth and shook her head violently No at him. The boy snuffled loudly and ducked his head.

'Need a tissue, William Ernest?' Trotter pulled one from her apron pocket and gently wiped his nose. 'And here's a clean one for school, honey.' Trotter leaned over and tucked a tissue into his pants pocket.

Gilly craned her neck over the table as though she were trying to see the contents of W.E.'s pocket. Her head was within a couple of feet of Trotter's eyes. The woman was sure to notice.

'William Ernest got promoted to the Orange reading group yesterday. Didn't you, William Ernest, honey?'

The little boy nodded his head but kept his eyes on his bowl.

'You're gonna have to do some reading out loud and show Gilly how great you're coming along with your reading these days.'

W.E. looked up for one split second with terror in his eyes. Trotter missed the look, but not Gilly, who smiled widely and shook her half-bulldozed head emphatically.

'In Orange they use hardback books,' Trotter was explaining. 'It's a real big step to be Orange.' She leaned over Gilly to put some toast on the table. 'We really worked for this.'

'So old W.E.'s getting a *head*, is he?'

Trotter gave her a puzzled look. 'Yeah, he's doing just fine.'

'Before you know it,' Gilly heard herself saying loudly, 'he'll be blowing his own nose and *combing his own hair*.'

'He already does,' said Trotter quietly. 'Leastways most of the time.' She sat down with a loud sigh at the table. 'Pass me a piece of toast, will you, Gilly?'

Gilly picked up the plate, raised it to the height of her hair, and passed it across to Trotter at that level.

'Thank you, honey.'

At eight thirty Trotter got William Ernest off to school. Gilly had long since finished her breakfast, but she sat at the kitchen table, her head propped on her fists. From the doorway she could hear Old Mother Goose honking over her gosling. 'OK, Big Orange, you show 'em down there today, hear?' Trotter said finally; and then the heavy door shut and she was heading back for the kitchen. As she got to the door, Gilly sat up straight and shook her head for all she was'worth.

'You got a tic or something, honey?'

'No.'

'I would've thought you was too young for the palsy,' the huge woman murmured, sliding into her seat with the cup of coffee she'd promised herself earlier. 'I see you got sneakers. That's good. You're supposed to have them for gym. Can you think of anything else you'll need for school?'

Gilly shook her head, but halfheartedly. She was beginning to feel like an oversharpened pencil.

'I think I'll go upstairs till it's time,' she said.

'Oh, while you're up there, honey –'

'Yeah?' Gilly sprang to attention.

'Make the beds, will you? It does look messy to leave 'em unmade all day, and I'm not much on running up and down the stairs.'

Gilly banged the door to her room for all she was worth. She spit every obscenity she'd ever heard through her teeth, but it wasn't enough. That ignorant hippopotamus! That walrus-faced imbecile! That – that – oh, the devil – Trotter wouldn't even let a drop fall from her precious William Ernest baby's nose, but she would let Gilly go to school – a new school where she didn't know anybody – looking like a scarecrow. Miss Ellis would surely hear about this. Gilly slammed her fist into her pillow. There had to be a law against foster mothers who showed such gross favouritism.

Well, she would show that lard can a thing or two. She yanked open the left top drawer, pulling out a broken comb, which she viciously jerked through the wilderness on her head, only to be defeated by a patch of bubble gum. She ran into the bathroom and rummaged through the medicine chest until she found a pair of nail scissors with which to chop out the offending hair. When despite her assault by comb and scissors a few strands refused to lie down meekly, she soaked them mercilessly into submission. She'd show the world. She'd show them who Galadriel Hopkins was – she was not to be trifled with.

'I see they call you Gilly,' said Mr Evans, the principal.

'I can't even pronounce the poor child's real name,' said Trotter, chuckling in what she must believe was a friendly manner.

It didn't help Gilly's mood. She was still seething over the hair combing.

'Well, Gilly's a fine name,' said Mr Evans, which confirmed to Gilly that at school, too, she was fated to be surrounded by fools.

The principal was studying records that must have been sent over from Gilly's former school, Hollywood Gardens Elementary. He coughed several times. 'Well,' he said, 'I think this young lady needs to be in a class that will challenge her.'

'She's plenty smart, if that's what you mean.'

Trotter, you dummy. How do you know how smart I am? You never laid eyes on me until yesterday.

'I'm going to put you into Miss Harris's class. We have some departmentalization in the sixth grade, but...'

'You got *what* in the sixth grade?'

Oh, Trotter, shut your fool mouth.

But the principal didn't seem to notice what a dope Trotter was. He explained patiently how some of the sixth-grade classes moved around for math and reading and science, but Miss Harris kept the same group all day.

What a blinking bore.

They went up three flights of ancient stairway to Miss Harris's room slowly, so that Trotter would not collapse.

The corridors stank of oiled floors and cafeteria soup. Gilly had thought she hated all schools so much that they no longer could pain or disappoint her, but she felt heavier with each step – like a condemned prisoner walking an endless last mile.

They paused before the door marked 'Harris–6'. Mr Evans knocked, and a tall tea-coloured woman, crowned with a bush of black hair, opened the door. She smiled down on the three of them, because she was even taller than the principal.

Gilly shrank back, bumping into Trotter's huge breast, which made her jump forward again quickly. God, on top of everything else, the teacher was black.

No one seemed to take notice of her reaction, unless you counted a flash of brightness in Miss Harris's dark eyes.

Trotter patted Gilly's arm, murmured something that ended in 'honey', and then she and the principal floated backward, closing Gilly into Harris–6. The teacher led her to an empty desk in the middle of the classroom, asked for Gilly's jacket, which she handed over to another girl to hang on the coatrack at the back of the room. She directed Gilly to sit down, and then went up and settled herself at the large teacher's desk to glance through the handful of papers Mr Evans had given her.

In a moment she looked up, a warm smile lighting her face. 'Galadriel Hopkins. What a beautiful name! From Tolkien, of course.'

'No,' muttered Gilly. 'Hollywood Gardens.'

Miss Harris laughed a sort of golden laugh. 'No, I mean your name – Galadriel. It's the name of a great queen in a book by a man named Tolkien. But, of course, you know that.'

Hell. No one had ever told her that her name came from a book. Should she pretend she knew all about it or play dumb?

'I'd like to call you Galadriel, if you don't mind. It's such a lovely name.'

'No!' Everyone was looking at Gilly peculiarly. She must have yelled louder than she intended to. 'I would prefer,' she said tightly, 'to be called Gilly.'

'Yes' – Miss Harris's voice was more steel than gold now – 'Yes. Gilly, it is then. Well' – she turned her smile on the rest of the class – 'Where were we?'

The clamour of their answers clashed in Gilly's brain. She started to put her head down on the desk, but someone was shoving a book into her face.

It wasn't fair – nothing was fair. She had once seen a picture in an old book of a red fox on a high rock surrounded by snarling dogs. It was like that. She was smarter than all of them, but they were too many. They had her surrounded, and in their stupid ways, they were determined to wear her down.

Miss Harris was leaning over her. Gilly pulled away as far as she could.

'Did you do division with fractions at Hollywood Gardens?'

Gilly shook her head. Inside she seethed. It was bad enough having to come to this broken-down old school but to be behind – to seem dumber than the rest of the kids – to have to appear a fool in front of . . . Almost half the class was black. And she would look dumb to *them*. A bunch of –

'Why don't you bring your chair up to my desk, and we'll work on it?'

Gilly snatched up her chair and beat Miss Harris to the front of the room. She'd show them!

At recesstime Monica Bradley, one of the other white girls in the class, was supposed to look after her on the playground. But Monica was more interested in leaning against the building and talking with her friends, which she did, keeping her back toward Gilly as she giggled and gossiped with two other sixth-grade girls, one of whom was black with millions of tiny braids all over her head. Like some African bushwoman. Not that Gilly cared. Why should she? They could giggle their stupid lives away, and she'd never let it bother her. She turned her back on them. That would show them.

Just then a ball jerked loose from the basketball game nearby and rushed toward her. She grabbed it. Balls were friends. She hugged it and ran over to the basket and threw it up, but she had been in too much of a hurry. It kissed the rim but refused to go in for her. Angrily she jumped and caught it before it bounced. She was dimly aware of a protest from the players, but they were boys and mostly shorter than she, so not worthy of notice. She shot again, this time with care. It arched and sank cleanly. She pushed someone out of the way and grabbed it just below the net.

'Hey! Who you think you are?'

One of the boys, a black as tall as she, tried to pull the ball from her hands. She spun round, knocking him to the concrete, and shot again, banking the ball off the back-board neatly into the net. She grabbed it once more.

Now all the boys were after her. She began to run across the playground laughing and clutching the ball to her chest. She could hear the boys screaming behind her, but she was too fast for them. She ran in and out of hopscotch games and right through a jump rope, all the way back to the basketball post where she shot again, missing wildly in her glee.

The boys did not watch for the rebound. They leaped upon her. She was on her back, scratching and kicking for all she was worth. They were yelping like hurt puppies.

'Hey! Hey! What's going on here?'

Miss Harris towered above them. The fighting evaporated under her glare. She marched all seven of them to the principal's office. Gilly noted with satisfaction a long red line down the tall boy's cheek. She'd actually drawn blood in the fracas. The boys looked a lot worse than she felt. Six to one – pretty good odds even for the great Gilly Hopkins.

Mr Evans lectured the boys about fighting on the playground and then sent them back to their homerooms. He kept Gilly longer.

'Gilly.' He said her name as though it were a whole sentence by itself. Then he just sat back in his chair, his fingertips pressed together, and looked at her.

She smoothed her hair and waited, staring him in the eye. People hated that – you staring them down as though they were the ones who had been bad. They didn't know how to deal with it. Sure enough. The principal looked away first.

'Would you like to sit down?'

She jerked her head No.

He coughed. 'I would rather for us to be friends.'

Gilly smirked.

'We're not going to have fighting on the playground.' He looked directly at her. 'Or anywhere else around here. I think you need to understand that, Gilly.'

She tilted her head sassily and kept her eyes right on his.

'You're at a new school now. You have a chance to – uh – make a new start. If you want to.'

So Hollywood Gardens had warned him, eh? Well, so what? The people here would have learned soon enough. Gilly would have made sure of that.

She smiled what she knew to be her most menacing smile.

'If there's anyway I can help you – if you just feel like talking to somebody...'

Not one of those understanding adults. Deliver me! She smiled so hard it stretched the muscles around her eyes. 'I'm OK,' she said. 'I don't need any help.'

'If you don't want help, there's no way I can make you accept it. But, Gilly' – he leaned forward in his chair and spoke very slowly and softly – 'you're not going to be permitted to hurt other people.'

She snuffled loudly. Cute. Very cute.

He leaned back; she thought she heard him sigh. 'Not if I have anything to do with it.'

Gilly wiped her nose on the back of her hand. She saw the principal half reach for his box of tissues and then pull his hand back.

'You may go back to your class now.' She turned to go. 'I hope you'll give yourself – and us – a chance, Gilly.'

She ignored the remark. Nice, she thought, climbing the dark stairs. Only a half day and already the principal was yo-yoing. Give her a week, boy. A week and she'd have the whole cussed place in an uproar. But this afternoon, she'd cool it a little. Let them worry. Then tomorrow or maybe even the next day, *Wham*. She felt her old powers returning. She was no longer tired.

# 'Sarsaparilla to Sorcery'

She met Agnes Stokes the next day at recess. Agnes was a shrivelled-up-looking little sixth grader from another class. She had long red hair that fell rather greasily to her waist, and when she sidled up to Gilly on the playground, the first thing Gilly noticed was how dirty her fingernails were.

'I know who you are,' the girl said. For a moment Gilly was reminded of the story of Rumpelstiltskin. Like that little creature, this girl had power over her. She knew who Gilly was, but Gilly didn't know who she was.

'Yeah?' said Gilly to let the evil little dwarf know that she wasn't interested.

'That was great about you beating up six boys yesterday.'

'Yeah?' Gilly couldn't help but be a little interested.

'It's all over the school.'

'So?'

'So.' The girl leaned against the building beside her, as though assuming Gilly would be pleased with her company.

'So?'

The girl twitched her freckled nose. 'I thought me and you should get together.'

'How come?' Rumpelstiltskins were always after something.

'No reason.' The smaller girl had on a jacket the sleeves of which were so long that they came down to her knuckles. She began to roll up first her left sleeve and then her right. She did it slowly and silently, as though it were part of some ceremony. It gave Gilly the creeps.

'What's your name?' Gilly blurted out the question, half expecting the girl to refuse to answer.

'Agnes Stokes' – she lowered her voice conspiratorily – 'You can call me Ag.'

Big deal. She was glad when the bell rang, and she could leave Agnes Stokes behind. But when she left school that afternoon, Agnes slipped out from the corner of the building and fell in step with her.

'Wanta come over?' she asked. 'My grandma won't care.'

'Can't.' Gilly had no intention of going into Agnes Stokes's house until she found out what Agnes Stokes was up to. People like Agnes Stokes didn't try to make friends without a reason.

She walked faster, but Agnes kept up with funny, little skip steps. When they got all the way up the hill to Trotter's house, Agnes actually started up the walk after Gilly.

Gilly turned around fiercely. 'You can't come in today!'

'How come?'

'Because,' said Gilly, 'I live with a terrible ogre that eats up little redheaded girls in one gulp.'

Agnes stepped back, with a startled look on her face. 'Oh,' she said. Then she giggled nervously. 'I get it. You're teasing.'

'*Arum golly goshee labooooooo!*' screamed Gilly, bearing down on the smaller girl like a child-eating giant.

Agnes backed away. 'Wha – ?'

Good. She had succeeded in unsettling Rumpelstiltskin. 'Maybe tomorrow,' said Gilly calmly and marched into the house without turning around.


'That you, William Ernest, honey?'

It made her want to puke the way Trotter carried on over that little weirdo.

Trotter came into the hall. 'Oh, Gilly,' she said. 'You got home so quick today I thought it was William Ernest.'

'Yeah.' Gilly started past her up the stairs.

'Wait a minute, honey. You got some mail.'

Mail! It could only be from – and it was. She snatched it out of Trotter's puffy fingers and raced up the stairs, slamming the door and falling upon the bed in one motion. It was a postcard showing sunset on the ocean. Slowly she turned it over.

> My dearest Galadriel,
>
> The agency wrote me that you had moved.
> I wish it were to here. I miss you.
>
> All my love, Courtney

That was all. Gilly read it again. And then a third time. No. That was not all. Up on the address side, in the left-hand corner. The letters were squeezed together so you could hardly read them. An address. Her mother's address.

She could go there. She could hitchhike across the country to California. She would knock on the door, and her mother would open it. And Courtney would throw her arms around her and kiss her all over her face and never let her go. 'I wish it were to here. I miss you.' See, Courtney wanted her to come. 'All my love.'

Inside her head, Gilly packed the brown suitcase and crept down the stairs. It was the middle of the night. Out into the darkness. No. She shivered a little. She would pick a time when Trotter was fussing over W.E. or Mr Randolph. She'd steal some food. Maybe a little money. People picked up hitchhikers all the time. She'd get to California in a few days. Probably less than a week. People were always picking up hitchhikers. And beating them up. And killing them. And pitching their dead bodies into the woods. All because she didn't have any money to buy a plane ticket or even a bus ticket.

Oh, why did it have to be so hard? Other kids could be with their mothers all the time. Dumb, stupid kids who didn't even like their mothers much. While she –

She put her head down and began to cry. She didn't mean to, but it was so unfair. She hadn't even seen her mother since she was three years old. Her beautiful mother who missed her so much and sent her all her love.

'You all right, honey?' Tap, tap, tap. 'You all right?'

Gilly sat up straight. Couldn't anyone have any privacy around this dump? She stuffed the postcard under her pillow and then smoothed the covers that she'd refused to straighten before school. She stood up at the end of the bed like a soldier on inspection. But the door didn't open.

'Anything I can do for you, honey?'

Yeah. Fry yourself, lard face.

'Can I come in?'

'No!' shrieked Gilly, then snatched open the door. 'Can't you leave me alone for one stupid minute?'

Trotter's eyelids flapped on her face like shutters on a vacant house. 'You OK, honey?' she repeated.

'I will be soon as you get your fat self outta here!'

'OK.' Trotter backed up slowly toward the stairs. 'Call me, if you want anything.' As an afterthought, she said, 'It ain't a shameful thing to need help, you know.'

'I don't need any help' – Gilly slammed the door, then yanked it open – 'from anybody!' She slammed it shut once more.

'I miss you. All my love.' I don't need help from anybody except from you. If I wrote you – if I asked, would you come and get me? You're the only one in the world I need. I'd be good for you. You'd see. I'd change into a whole new person. I'd turn from gruesome Gilly into gorgeous, gracious, good, glorious Galadriel. And grateful. Oh, Courtney – oh, Mother, I'd be so grateful.

\*

'Lord, you are so good to us.' Mr Randolph was saying the supper blessing. 'Yes, Lord, so very good. We have this wonderful food to eat and wonderful friends to enjoy it with. Now, bless us, Lord, and make us truly, truly grateful. Ah-men.'

'Ay-men. My, Mr Randolph, you do ask a proper blessing.'

'Oh, Mrs Trotter, when I sit before the spread of your table, I got so much to be thankful for.'

Good lord, how was a person supposed to eat through this garbage?

'Well, Miss Gilly, how was school for you today?'

Gilly grunted. Trotter gave her a sharp look. 'It was OK, I guess.'

'My, you young people have such a wonderful opportunity today. Back when I was going to school – oh, thank you, Mrs Trotter – what a delicious-smelling plate. My, my...'

To Gilly's relief, the blind man's attention was diverted from his tale of childhood schooldays to the organization of the food on his plate and the eating of it, which he did with a constant murmuring of delight, dropping little bits from his mouth to his chin or tie.

Disgusting. Gilly switched her attention to William Ernest, who, as usual, was staring at her bug-eyed. She smiled primly and mouthed, 'How do you do, sweetums?'

Sweetums immediately choked on a carrot. He coughed until tears came.

'What's the matter, William Ernest, honey?'

'I think' – Gilly smiled her old lady principal smile – 'the dear child is choking. It must be something he ate.'

'Are you all right, baby?' asked Trotter.

W.E. nodded through his tears.

'Sure?'

'Maybe he needs a pat on the back,' Mr Randolph offered.

'Yeah!' said Gilly. 'How about it, W.E., old man? Want me to swat you one?'

'*No!* Don't let her hit me.'

'Nobody's gonna hit you, honey. Everybody just wants to help.' Trotter looked hard at Gilly. 'Right, Gilly?'

'Just want to help, little buddy.' Gilly flashed her crooked-politician smile.

'I'm all right,' the boy said in a small strangled voice. He slid his chair a couple of inches toward Trotter's end of the table, so that he was no longer directly across from Gilly.

'Say, W.E.' – Gilly flashed her teeth at him – 'how about you and me doing a little red-hot reading after supper? You know, squeeze the old orange reader?'

W.E. shook his head, his eyes pleading with Trotter to save him.

'My, oh, my, Mrs Trotter. I can tell how old I am when I can't even understand the language of the young people about me,' said Mr Randolph.

Trotter was looking first at W.E. and then at Gilly. 'Don't you fret yourself, Mr Randolph.' She leaned across the corner of the table and patted William Ernest gently, keeping her eyes on Gilly. 'Don't you fret, now. Sometimes these kids'll tease the buttons off a teddy bear. Ain't nothing to do with age.'

'Hell, I was just trying to help the kid,' muttered Gilly.

'He don't always know that,' Trotter said, but her eyes were saying 'like heck you were'. 'I got a real good idea,' she went on. 'They tell me, Gilly, that you are some kind of a great reader yourself. I know Mr Randolph would like to hear you read something.'

The little wrinkled face brightened. 'My, my! Would you do that, Miss Gilly? It would be such a pleasure to me.'

Trotter, you rat. 'I don't have anything to read,' Gilly said.

'OK, that ain't a problem. Mr Randolph's got enough books to start a public library, haven't you, Mr Randolph?'

'Well, I do have a few,' he chuckled. 'Course you've got the Good Book right here.'

'What good book?' demanded Gilly, interested in spite of herself. She did like a good book.

'I believe Mr Randolph is referring to the Holy Bible.'

'The *Bible*?' Gilly didn't know whether to laugh or cry. She had a vision of herself trapped forever in the dusty brown parlour reading the Bible to Trotter and Mr Randolph. She would read on and on forever, while the two of them nodded piously at each other. She jumped up from her chair. 'I'll get a book,' she said. 'I'll run over to Mr Randolph's and choose something.'

She was afraid they would try to stop her, force her to read the Bible, but they both seemed pleased and let her go.


Mr Randolph's front door was unlocked. The house was pitch-black and mustier than Trotter's. Quickly, Gilly pushed a light switch. Nothing happened. Of course. Why should Mr Randolph care if a bulb burned out? She stumbled from the hall to where she thought the living room should be, fumbling along the wall with her fingers until she found another switch. To her relief this one worked – only 40 watts' worth, maybe – but still there was light.

Leaning against two walls of the crowded little room were huge antique bookcases that reached the ceiling. And stacked or lying upside down, even put in backward, were books – hundreds of them. They looked old and thick with dust. It was hard to think of funny little Mr Randolph actually reading them. She wondered how long he had been blind. She wished she could push her mind past those blank white eyes into whatever of Mr Randolph all these books must represent.

She went toward the larger shelf to the right of the door, but she felt strangely shy about actually touching the books. It was almost as though she were meddling in another person's brain. Wait. Maybe they were all for show. Maybe Mr Randolph collected books, trying to act like some big-shot genius, even though he himself couldn't read a word. No one would ever catch on. They'd think he didn't read because he couldn't see. That was it, of course. She felt better. Now she was free to look at the books themselves.

Without thinking, she began to straighten out the shelves as she read the titles. She saw several volumes of an encyclopedia set: 'Antarctica to Balfe', then 'Jerez to Liberty'. She looked around for other volumes. It bothered her to have everything in a muddle. High on the top shelf was 'Sarsaparilla to Sorcery'. She dragged a heavy stuffed chair backward to the shelf and climbed up on the very top of its back. On tiptoe, leaning against the rickety lower shelves to keep from toppling, she could barely reach the book. She pulled at it with the tip of her fingers, catching it as it fell. Something fluttered to the floor as she did so.

Money. She half fell, half jumped off the chair, and snatched it up. Two five-dollar bills had fallen out from behind 'Sarsaparilla to Sorcery'. She put the encyclopedia down and studied the old, wrinkled bills. Just when she was needing money so badly. Here they'd come floating down. Like magic. Ten dollars wouldn't get her very far, but there might be more where these came from. She climbed up again, stretching almost to the point of falling, but it was no good. Although she could just about reach the top shelf with her fingertips, she was very unsteady, and the lower shelves were much too wobbly to risk climbing.

Heavy footsteps thudded across the front porch. The front door opened. 'You all right, Gilly, honey?'

Gilly nearly tripped over herself, leaping down and grabbing up 'Sarsaparilla to Sorcery' from the chair seat, stretching her guts out to tip the book into its place on the shelf. And just in time. She got down on the chair seat, as Trotter appeared at the door.

'You was taking so long,' she said. 'Then Mr Randolph remembered that maybe the bulbs was all burned out. He tends to forget since they really don't help him much.'

'There's a light here,' Gilly snapped. 'If there hadn't been, I'd have come back. I'm not retarded.'

'I believe you mentioned that before,' said Trotter dryly. 'Well, you find anything you wanted to read to Mr Randolph?'

'It's a bunch of junk.'

'One man's trash is another man's treasure,' Trotter said in a maddeningly calm voice, wandering over to a lower shelf as she did so. She pulled out a squat leatherbound volume and blew the dust off the top. 'He's got a yen for poetry, Mr Randolph does.' She handed the book up to Gilly, who was still perched on the chair. 'This is one I used to try to read to him last year, but' – her voice sounded almost shy – 'I ain't too hot a reader myself, as you can probably guess.'

Gilly stepped down. She was still angry with Trotter for bursting in on her, but she was curious to know just what sort of poetry old man Randolph fancied. *The Oxford Book of English Verse*. She flipped it open, but it was too dark to see the words properly.

'Ready to come along?'

'Yeah, yeah,' she replied impatiently. Holding her neck straight to keep from looking up at 'Sarsaparilla', she followed Trotter's bulk back to her house.

'What did you bring?' Mr Randolph's face looked like a

child's before a wrapped-up present. He was sitting right
at the edge of the big brown chair.

'*The Oxford Book of English Verse*,' Gilly mumbled.

He cocked his head. 'I beg your pardon?'

'The poems we was reading last year, Mr Randolph.'

Trotter had raised her voice as she always did speaking
to the old man.

'Oh, good, good,' he said, sliding back into the chair
until his short legs no longer touched the worn rug.

Gilly opened the book. She flipped through the junk at
the beginning and came to the first poem. 'Cuckoo Song,'
she read the title loudly. It was rather pleasant being able
to do something well that none of the rest of them could.
Then she glanced at the body of the poem.

> Sumer is icumen in,
>   Lhude sing cuccu!
> Groweth sed, and bloweth med,
>   And springth the wude nu –
>         Sing cuccu!

Cuckoo was right. 'Wait a minute,' she muttered, turning
the page.

> Bytuene Mershe ant Averil...

She looked quickly at the next.

> Lenten ys come with love to toune...

And the next –

> Ichot a burde in boure bryht,
>   That fully semly is on syht...

She slammed the book shut. They were obviously trying to
play a trick on her. Make her seem stupid. See, there was
Mr Randolph giggling to himself. 'It's not in English!' she
yelled. 'You're just trying to make a fool of me.'

'No, no, Miss Gilly. Nobody's trying to make a fool of you. The real old English is at the front. Try over a way.'

'You want the Wordsworth one, Mr Randolph?' asked Trotter. 'Or do you have that by heart?'

'Both,' he said happily.

Trotter came over and leaned across Gilly, who was sitting on the piano bench. 'I can find it,' said Gilly, pulling the book out of her reach. 'Just tell me the name of it.'

'William Wordsworth,' said Mr Randolph. 'There was a time when meadow, grove, and stream...' He folded his small hands across his chest, his voice no longer pinched and polite, but soft and warm.

Gilly found the page and began to read:

> 'There was a time when meadow, grove, and stream,
> The earth, and every common sight,
>     To me did seem
>     Apparell'd in celestial light,
> The glory and the freshness of a dream.'

She stopped a minute as though to listen to her own echo.

'It is not now...' Mr Randolph's velvet voice prompted her.

> 'It is not now as it hath been of yore: —
>     Turn wheresoe'er I may,
>         By night or day...'

Leaning against the back of the chair, Mr Randolph joined and with one voice they recited:

> 'The things which I have seen I now can see no more.'

They continued to read that way. He would listen blissfully for a while and then join, turning her single voice into the sound of a choir.

She read:

> 'Our birth is but a sleep and a forgetting:
> The Soul that rises with us, our life's Star,

> Hath had elsewhere its setting,
>    And cometh from afar:
> Not in entire forgetfulness,
>    And not in utter nakedness . . .'

And then together

> 'But trailing clouds of glory do we come
>    From God, who is our home . . .'

'Trailing clouds of glory do we come.' The music of the words rolled up and burst across Gilly like waves upon a beach.

It was a long poem. Seven pages or so of small print. She couldn't understand really what it meant. But Mr Randolph seemed to know each word, prompting her gently if she started to stumble on an unfamiliar one, and joining her, powerfully and musically, on his own favourite lines.

They chorused the final lines:

> 'Thanks to the human heart by which we live,
> Thanks to its tenderness, its joys, and fears,
> To me the meanest flower that blows can give
> Thoughts that do often lie too deep for tears.'

Mr Randolph gave a long sigh. 'Thank you, thank you,' he said softly.

'She's a handsome reader, all right.' Trotter was smiling proudly as though she might share the credit for Gilly's talent.

The smile irritated Gilly. She was a good reader because she had set her mind to be one. The minute that damn first-grade teacher had told Mrs Dixon that she was afraid Gilly might be 'slow', Gilly had determined to make the old parrot choke on her crackers. And she had. By Christmastime she was reading circles around the whole snotty class. Not that it made any difference. The teacher, Mrs

Gorman, had then explained very carefully to Mrs Dixon that she had twenty-five other children to look out for and that there was no way to set up a private reading time for one individual. Gilly would just have to learn some patience and cooperation. That was all.

'Well, what do you think of Mr Wordsworth, Miss Gilly?' asked Mr Randolph, interrupting her angry thoughts.

'Stupid,' she said to the memory of Mrs Gorman rather than to him.

A look of pain crossed his face. 'I suppose,' he said in his pinched, polite voice, 'in just one reading, one might...'

'Like here' – Gilly now felt forced to justify an opinion which she didn't in the least hold– 'like here at the end, "the meanest flower that blows". What in the hell – what's that supposed to mean? Whoever heard of a "mean flower"?'

Mr Randolph relaxed. 'The word *mean* has more than one definition, Miss Gilly. Here the poet is talking about humility, lowliness, not' – he laughed softly – 'not bad nature.'

Gilly flushed. 'I never saw a flower blow, either.'

'Dandelions.' They all turned to look at William Ernest, not only startled by the seldom-heard sound of his voice, but by the fact that all three had forgotten that he was even in the room. There he sat, cross-legged on the floor at the end of the couch, a near-sighted guru, blinking behind his glasses.

'You hear that?' Trotter's voice boomed with triumph. 'Dandelions? Ain't that the smartest thing you ever heard? Ain't it?'

W.E. ducked his head behind the cover of the couch arm.

'That is probably exactly the flower that Mr Wordsworth meant,' Mr Randolph said. 'Surely it is the lowliest flower of all.'

'Meanest flower there is,' agreed Trotter happily. 'And they sure do blow, just like William Ernest says. They blow all over the place.' She turned toward Gilly as though for agreement, but at the sight of Gilly's face, the woman's smile stuck.

'Can I go now?' Gilly's voice was sharp like the jagged edge of a tin-can top.

Trotter nodded. 'Sure,' she said quietly.

'I do appreciate more than you know –' but Gilly didn't wait to hear Mr Randolph's appreciation. She ran up the stairs into her room. Behind the closed door, she pulled the two bills from her pocket, and lying on the bed, smoothed out the wrinkles. She would hide them beneath her underwear until she could figure out a better place, and tomorrow she would call the bus station and ask the price of a one-way ticket to San Francisco.

'I'm coming, Courtney,' she whispered. 'Trailing clouds of glory as I come.'

It was only a matter of getting back into Mr Randolph's house and getting the rest of the money. There was sure to be more.

# William Ernest
# and Other Mean Flowers

Agnes Stokes was waiting outside when she started for school the next morning. Gilly's first impulse was to turn around and go back into the house until Agnes had left, but it was too late. Agnes was already waving and yelling to her. What a creep! Gilly walked past her quickly without speaking. She could hear Agnes's little scurrying steps behind her; then there was a dirty hand on her arm.

Disgusted, Gilly shook it off.

Agnes's hand was gone, but she hooked her chin over Gilly's upper arm, her face twisted up to look Gilly in the face. Her breath smelled. 'What are we going to do today?' she asked.

We? Are you kidding?

'Want to fight the boys again? I'll help.'

Gilly spun around and brought her nose down close to Agnes's stubby one. Ugh. 'When are you gonna get it through that ant brain of yours that *I don't want help*?'

Agnes withdrew her nose and shook her greasy hair, but to Gilly's annoyance she clung like a louse nit, scurrying beside Gilly, two or three little steps to every one of Gilly's.

Though it was hard to ignore her the rest of the way to the school, Gilly managed by putting on her celebrity-in-a-parade face, staring glassy-eyed far into the crowd, blanking out everything within close range.

'I just live up the next block from you, you know.'

Thrillsville.

'I'll stop by for you every day, OK?'

The little jerk couldn't even figure out that she was being ignored.

Just as they reached the schoolyard, Agnes waved a large unwrapped piece of gum before Gilly's nose. 'Want some bubble gum?'

Oh, what the heck. The queen had used Rumpelstiltskin, hadn't she? Agnes might come in handy some day. The trick was in knowing how to dispose of people when you were through with them, and Gilly had had plenty of practice performing that trick.

She took the gum without speaking. Agnes flushed with pleasure. 'See that kid over by the fence? The one with the big nose? Her mother run away with a sailor last May.'

'So?'

Agnes put her hand up and whispered behind it. 'My grandma says the whole family's nothing but trash.'

'Yeah?' Gilly smacked her gum noisily. 'What's your grandma say about your family?'

Agnes went as stiff as a dried sponge. 'Who's been telling lies about my family?'

'Lucky guess.'

'They're coming back. Both of them.'

'Sure.'

'Well, they are. Probably before Christmas.'

'OK, OK, I believe you.'

Agnes's eyes darted back and forth in their sockets, studying Gilly's expressionless face. 'Are you making fun of me?' she asked finally.

'I wouldn't do that.'

Agnes's uncertainty wavered. 'I know a lot more stuff,' she said. 'You know – junk about people around here.'

'I bet you do, sweetheart.' Gilly carefully blew a medium-sized bubble which popped dangerously close to Agnes's stringy red hair.

Agnes let out a sharp little laugh. 'Watch it!' she said nervously. The first bell rang. 'See you at recess?'

Gilly shrugged and headed for Harris 6. 'Maybe,' she said.

Although a part of Gilly's head wanted to get on with her schemes of how to get Mr Randolph's money, once she crossed the threshold of Harris 6, she forced herself to concentrate on her lessons. She had made up her mind that first day to pay attention in Miss Harris's class. She wasn't going to let a bunch of low-class idiots think they were smarter than she was. It was infuriating to find herself behind in almost every subject, but she knew that the fault lay in Hollywood Gardens Elementary and not in herself. She would work madly until she had not only caught up with but passed them all, and then she'd skid to a total halt. That kind of technique drove teachers wild. They took it personally when someone who could obviously run circles around the rest of the class completely refused to play the game. Yep. And in Miss Harris's case that was just how Gilly wanted it taken.

At lunchtime Agnes's class had gotten to the cafeteria first, so when Gilly left the line, Agnes was already seated and waved her over to her table. Gilly would have preferred to eat alone. Agnes wasn't the most appetizing luncheon companion, but since Gilly had decided Agnes might sometime come in handy, she might as well get used to her. She went over and sat down opposite Agnes, who smiled like a cartoon cat across the trays. 'I get free lunch, too,' she said.

Gilly glared at her. Nobody was supposed to know who got free lunch and who didn't. So much for privacy. The first thing she was going to teach Agnes Stokes was when to keep her big mouth shut.

'You know, don't you, Agnes, it makes me sick just looking at you?'

Agnes gave her kicked-dog expression. 'Wha' cha mean?'

'Nothing personal. You just make me sick – that's all.'

Agnes jerked the cafeteria bench closer to the table and started to roll up her dragging shirtsleeves.

'It's nothing personal,' Gilly continued. 'In fact, you probably can't help it. I don't blame you. I'm just not going to put up with it.'

'Put up with what?'

Gilly leaned way across the table and right into Agnes's pink face. 'Your big mouth!'

Agnes tilted backward to get her face out of Gilly's leering one. People were staring at them. They both straightened up, but Gilly kept the leer in place.

'I ain't got no big mouth,' Agnes said quietly.

'Then keep it shut. We wouldn't want what's left of your brains to trickle out.'

Agnes's mouth flew open and immediately slammed shut. She shrugged, gave an angry little sniff, and then began to eat her lunch.

Gilly paused to give a generous smile to the other people at the table while spreading her napkin delicately on her lap and picking up the milk carton with her pinky curled the way Mrs Nevins used to do when she picked up her coffee cup.

After lunch she allowed Agnes to follow her around the playground like a stray puppy. Once Agnes ventured a tentative 'Hey, Gil,' but Gilly spun around with such a frightening look that any further words withered.

And when Gilly left school, Agnes fell in behind her without a word. They marched up the hill, Agnes tripping along double time to keep up with Gilly's exaggerated strides. When they got to Trotter's, Gilly went in. As she was closing the dirty white picket gate behind her, Agnes touched her arm and handed her a note. It said: 'When can I talk?'

Gilly smiled benignly. 'We'll see,' she said. 'We'll just see how it goes.'

Agnes opened her mouth like a starved baby bird, but she didn't give a chirp. Good bird. Gilly patted the skinny, freckled arm and swept up the walk into the house, leaving the open-mouthed fledgling outside the gate.

'Zat you, William Ernest, honey?'

'Zat's me, Maime Trotter, baby,' squeaked Gilly.

From the kitchen she could hear Trotter's laugh rumbling. 'C'mon in here and get yourself a snack, Gilly, honey.'

Gilly was tempted, but determined not to yield. She was too smart to be bought with food, no matter how hungry she felt. She stomped up the stairs past the open kitchen door from which came the definite smell of chocolate chip cookies. Double-damn you, Maime Trotter.

Later, behind her carefully closed door, Gilly took out the money from the bureau. Then she pulled out the whole drawer and dumped it upside down on the bed. She smoothed out the bills on the drawer bottom, and then took from her pocket the masking tape she'd taken care to steal from Miss Harris's desk and taped the bills to the bottom of the drawer.

Without warning, the door flew open. Gilly, to cover the money, fell chest down over the drawer.

A frog-eyed William Ernest stood on the threshold, trying to juggle a small tray which held a plate of cookies and a glass of milk.

'What in the devil?' screeched Gilly.

'Tr-tr-tr-tr-Trotter . . .' was all the child could manage in the way of an answer. He was rattling the tray so hard that the milk glass was threatening to jump the edge.

'Well, put 'em down, stupid.'

W.E.'s eyes searched the room in desperation. Gilly was beginning to feel like a fool lying chest down on a bureau drawer. She raised herself enough to turn the drawer over. Then she sat up and turned to face him.

'Didn't Trotter ever tell you about knocking before you bust in?'

He nodded, eyes wide, tray rattling.

She sighed. What a weird little kid. 'OK,' she said, reaching out across the narrow space. 'Give it here.'

He shoved it at her and ran blamety-blam down the stairs. Gilly turned the drawer back over to make a table on the bed and put the milk and cookies on it. She shut the door and then sat down cross-legged on the bed and began to eat. Oh, thank you, thank you, Maime Trotter. What a delicious-smelling plate of cookies. My, my, and ahhhhh-men.

In the middle of the last cookie, an inspiration came to her. It wasn't Agnes Stokes whom she would use. Agnes couldn't be trusted between freckles. It was William Ernest. Of course. Trotter's honey baby engaged in a life of crime. She laughed out loud at the pleasure of it. Baby-Face Teague, the frog-eyed filcher. Wild-eyed William, the goose-brained godfather. The possibilities were unlimited and delectable. The midget of the Mafia. The Orange Read Squeezer. No. The Orange Squirt.

She jumped up and put the room to order, danced down the stairs, balancing the tray high on one hand, and skipped into the kitchen.

Trotter looked up from the table where she was spooning cookie dough onto a baking sheet and gave her the eye. 'Feeling good, now?'

Gilly gave her the 300-watt smile that she had designed especially for melting the hearts of foster parents. 'Never better!' She spoke the words with just the right musical lilt. She put her dishes by the sink, started to wash them but thought better of it. Trotter might get suspicious if goodness was overdone.

She skated out into the hall and around the bottom of the stairs right into the living room where W.E. sat on the floor staring at *Sesame Street*. She slid down beside him, and when his eyes checked her out sideways, she gave a quiet, sisterly kind of smile and pretended to be enthralled with Big Bird. She said nothing through *Sesame Street*, *Mr Roger's Neighborhood*, and *The Electric Company* but occasionally hummed along with one of the songs in a friendly sort of way, never failing to smile at William when she caught him snatching a quick stare in her direction.

Her strategy seemed to be succeeding. At any rate when suppertime neared, she said to him, 'Do you want to set the table or get Mr Randolph?' and he answered with hardly a stutter, 'Get Mr Randolph.'

So she set the kitchen table, humming under her breath the 'Sunny Days' theme from *Sesame Street*. And after supper she folded an airplane for him from notebook paper, and at her suggestion he even followed her out on the front porch to fly it.

W.E. squinched his little near-sighted eyes together, wrinkled up his stubby nose, drew his arm way back, and pitched the airplane with all his might. '*Pow*,' he whispered. The plane swooped down off the porch, then suddenly caught an updraught and climbed higher than their heads, looped and glided smoothly to the grass.

He turned shining eyes on her. 'See that?' he asked softly. 'See that?'

'OK, OK.' Gilly ran out and picked up the plane. It was the best one she'd ever made. She clambered up on the concrete post that held the porch railing in place and raised her arm. Then she thought better of it. 'You do it, William Ernest, OK?'

She climbed down and gave him a boost up. He seemed a little unsteady from the height of the post, glancing down, apparently afraid to move his feet.

'Look, I'm not going to let you fall, man.' She put her hands loosely around his ankles. She could feel him relaxing under her fingers. He reared back and shot. '*Pow*,' he said a little louder than before, sending the white craft with its pale blue lines as high – well, almost as high – as the house, looping, climbing, gliding, resting at last in the azalea bush in Mr Randolph's yard.

William Ernest scrambled off the post and down the steps. He was slowed by the fence, but not stopped. You could tell he'd never climbed a fence in his life, and it would have been faster by far to go through the gate and around, but he had chosen the most direct route to his precious plane.

He fell in Mr Randolph's yard in such a way that one arm and leg seemed to arrive before the other pair, but he picked himself up at once and delicately plucked his prize from the bush. He turned around to grin shyly at Gilly and then, as though carrying the crown of England, came down Mr Randolph's walk, the sidewalk, and into Trotter's gate.

About halfway up the walk, he said something.

'What you say?' Gilly asked.

'I say' – the veins on his neck stuck out with the effort of raising his voice to an audible level – 'I say, It sure fly good.'

He wasn't as dumb as he looked now, was he? thought Gilly smiling, without taking time to calculate which of her smiles to put on. 'You throw good, too, William E.'

'I do?'

'Sure. I was just admiring your style. I guess you've had lessons.'

He cocked his head in puzzlement.

'No? You just taught yourself?'

He nodded his head solemnly.

'Gee, man, you're a natural. I've never seen such a natural.'

He straightened his thin shoulders and marched up the stairs as though he were the President of the United States.

They were still flying the plane, or rather W.E. was flying it with Gilly looking on and making admiring remarks from time to time, when Trotter and Mr Randolph came out on the porch.

'You gotta see this, Trotter. William Ernest can do this really good.'

W.E. climbed unassisted to the top of the concrete post. He didn't need Gilly's hands or help now. 'Watch,' he said softly. 'Watch here.'

Mr Randolph lifted his sightless face upward. 'What is it, son?'

'Gilly made him a paper airplane, looks like,' interpreted Trotter.

'Oh, I see, I see.'

'Watch now.'

'We're watching, William Ernest, honey.'

W.E. leaned back and let fly – '*pow*' – for another swooping, soaring, slowly spiralling, skimming superflight.

Trotter sighed as the plane gracefully landed by the curb. William Ernest rushed to retrieve it.

'How was it?' Mr Randolph asked.

'I 'clare, Mr Randolph, sometimes it's a pity you gotta miss seeing things. I never thought paper airplanes was for anything but to drive teachers crazy before.' She turned to Gilly. 'That was really something,' she said.

Gilly could feel herself blushing, but W.E. came up the steps and saved her. 'It's 'cause I fly it so good,' he said.

'Yeah,' said Gilly, patting his shoulder. 'You sure do.' He looked up into her face, his squinty little eyes full of pure pleasure.

'Thank you,' said Trotter softly.

For a moment Gilly looked at her, then quickly turned

away as a person turns from bright sunlight. 'Want me to walk Mr Randolph home?' she asked.

'Thank you, Miss Gilly. I would appreciate that so much.'

She took his elbow and guided him carefully down the stairs, taking care not to look back over her shoulder because the look on Trotter's face was the one Gilly had, in some deep part of her, longed to see all her life, but not from someone like Trotter. That was not part of the plan.

# Harassing Miss Harris

By the third week in October, Gilly had caught up with her class and gone on ahead. She tried to tell herself that she had forced Miss Harris into a corner from which the woman could give her nothing but A's. Surely, it must kill old priss face to have to put rave notices – 'Excellent' 'Good, clear thinking' 'Nice Work' – on the papers of someone who so obviously disliked her.

But Miss Harris was a cool customer. If she knew that Gilly despised her, she never let on. So at this point Gilly was not ready to pull her time-honoured trick of stopping work just when the teacher had become convinced that she had a bloody genius on her hands. That had worked so beautifully at Hollywood Gardens – the whole staff had gone totally ape when suddenly one day she began turning in blank sheets of paper. It was the day after Gilly had overheard the principal telling her teacher that Gilly had made the highest score in the entire school's history on her national aptitude tests, but, of course, no one knew that she knew, so an army of school psychologists had been called in to try to figure her out. Since no one at school would take the blame for Gilly's sudden refusal to achieve, they decided to blame her foster parents, which made Mrs Nevins so furious that she demanded that Miss Ellis remove Gilly at once instead of waiting out the year – the year Mrs Nevins had reluctantly agreed to, after her first complaints about Gilly's sassy and underhanded ways.

But something warned Gilly that Miss Harris was not likely to crumble at the sight of a blank sheet of paper. She was more likely simply to ignore it. She was different from the other teachers Gilly had known. She did not appear to be dependent on her students. There was no evidence that they fed either her anxieties or her satisfactions. In Gilly's social-studies book there was a picture of a Muslim woman of Saudi Arabia, with her body totally covered except for her eyes. It reminded Gilly somehow of Miss Harris, who had wrapped herself up in invisible robes. Once or twice a flash in the eyes seemed to reveal something to Gilly of the person underneath the protective garments, but such flashes were so rare that Gilly hesitated to say even to herself what they might mean.

Some days it didn't matter to Gilly what Miss Harris was thinking or not thinking. It was rather comfortable to go to school with no one yelling or cajoling – to know that your work was judged on its merits and was not affected by the teacher's personal opinion of the person doing the work. It was a little like throwing a basketball. If you aimed right, you got it through the hoop; it was absolutely just and absolutely impersonal.

But other days, Miss Harris's indifference grated on Gilly. She was not used to being treated like everyone else. Ever since the first grade, she had forced her teachers to make a special case of her. She had been in charge of her own education. She had learned what and when it pleased her. Teachers had courted her and cursed her, but no one before had simply melted her into the mass.

As long as she had been behind the mass, she tolerated this failure to treat her in a special manner, but now, even the good-morning smile seemed to echo the math computer's 'Hello, Gilly number 58706, today we will continue our study of fractions.' *Crossing threshold of classroom causes auto-teacher to light up and say 'Good morning.' For three thousand dollars additional, get the personalized electric-eye model that calls each student by name.*

For several days she concentrated on the vision of a computer-activated Miss Harris. It seemed to fit. Brilliant, cold, totally, absolutely and maddeningly fair, all her inner workings shinily encased and hidden from view. Not a Muslim but a flawless tamperproof machine.

The more Gilly thought about it, the madder she got. No one had a right to cut herself off from other people like that. Just once, before she left this dump, she'd like to pull a wire inside that machine. Just once she'd like to see Harris 6 scream in anger – fall apart – break down.

But Miss Harris wasn't like Trotter. You didn't have to be around Trotter five minutes before you knew the direct route to her insides – William Ernest Teague. Miss Harris wasn't hooked up to other people. It was like old *Mission Impossible* reruns on TV: *Your mission, if you decide to accept it, is to get inside this computerized robot, discover how it operates, and neutralize its effectiveness.* The self-destructing tape never told the mission-impossible team how to complete their impossible mission, but the team always seemed to know. Gilly, on the other hand, hadn't a clue.

It was TV that gave her the clue. She hadn't been thinking about Miss Harris at all. She'd been thinking, actually, of how to get the rest of Mr Randolph's money and hadn't been listening to the news broadcast. Then somehow it began sending a message into her brain. A high government official had told a joke on an airplane that had gotten him fired. Not just any joke, mind you. A dirty joke. But that wasn't what got him fired. The dirty joke had been somehow insulting to blacks. Apparently all the black people in the country and even some whites were jumping up and down with rage. Unfortunately the commentator didn't repeat the joke. She could have used it. But at least she knew now something that might be a key to Harris 6.

She borrowed some money from Trotter for 'school supplies', and bought a pack of heavy white construction paper and magic markers. Behind the closed door of her bedroom she began to make a greeting card, fashioning it as closely as she could to the tall, thin, 'comic' cards on the special whirlaround stand in the drugstore.

At first she tried to draw a picture on the front, wasting five or six precious sheets of paper in the attempt. Cursing her incompetence, she stole one of Trotter's magazines and cut from it a picture of a tall, beautiful black woman in an Afro. Her skin was a little darker than Miss Harris's, but it was close enough.

Above the picture of the woman she lettered these words carefully (she could print well, even if her drawing stank):

They're saying 'Black is beautiful!'

Then below the picture:

But the best that I can figger
Is everyone who's saying so
Looks mighty like a

And inside in tiny letters:

person with a vested interest in
maintaining this point of view.

She had to admit it. It was about the funniest card she'd ever seen in her life. Gifted Gilly – a funny female of the first rank. If her bedroom had been large enough, she'd have rolled on the floor. As it was, she lay on the bed hugging herself and laughing until she was practically hysterical. Her only regret was that the card was to be anonymous. She would have enjoyed taking credit for this masterpiece.

She got to school very early the next morning and sneaked up the smelly stairs to Harris 6 before the janitor had even turned on the hall lights. For a moment she feared that the door might be locked, but it opened easily under her hand. She slipped the card into the math book that lay in the middle of Miss Harris's otherwise absolutely neat desk. She wanted to be sure that no one else would discover it and ruin everything.

All day long, but especially during math, Gilly kept stealing glances at Miss Harris. Surely at any minute, she would pick up the book. Surely she could see the end of the card sticking out and would be curious. But Miss Harris left the book exactly where it was. She borrowed a book from a student when she needed to refer to one. It was as though she sensed her own was booby-trapped.

By lunchtime Gilly's heart, which had started the day jumping with happy anticipation, was kicking angrily at her stomach. By midafternoon she was so mad that nothing had happened that she missed three spelling words, all of which she knew perfectly well. At the three o'clock bell, she slammed her chair upside down on her desk and headed for the door.

'Gilly.'

Her heart skipped as she turned toward Miss Harris.

'Will you wait a minute, please?'

They both waited, staring quietly at each other until the room emptied. Then Miss Harris got up from her desk and closed the door. She took a chair from one of the front desks and put it down a little distance from her own. 'Sit down for a minute, won't you?'

Gilly sat. The math book lay apparently undisturbed, the edge of the card peeping out at either end.

'You may find this hard to believe, Gilly, but you and I are very much alike.'

Gilly snapped to attention despite herself.

'I don't mean in intelligence, although that is true, too. Both of us are smart, and we know it. But the thing that brings us closer than intelligence is anger. You and I are two of the angriest people I know.' She said all this in a cool voice that cut each word in a thin slice from the next and then waited, as if to give Gilly a chance to challenge her. But Gilly was fascinated, like the guys in the movies watching the approach of a cobra. She wasn't about to make a false move.

'We do different things with our anger, of course. I was always taught to deny mine, which I did and still do. And that makes me envy you. Your anger is still up here on the surface where you can look it in the face, make friends with it if you want to.'

She might have been talking Swahili for all Gilly could understand.

'But I didn't ask you to stay after school to tell you how intelligent you are or how much I envy you, but to thank you for your card.'

It had to be sarcasm, but Harris-6 was smiling almost like a human being. When did the cobra strike?

'I took it to the teachers' room at noon and cursed creatively for twenty minutes. I haven't felt so good in years.'

She'd gone mad like the computer in *2001*. Gilly got up and started backing toward the door. Miss Harris just smiled and made no effort to stop her. As soon as she got to the stairs, Gilly began to run and, cursing creatively, ran all the way home.

# Dust and Desperation

All at once, leaving Thompson Park became urgent. Gilly knew in the marrow of her bones that if she stayed much longer, this place would mess her up. Between the craziness in the brown house and the craziness at school, she would become like W.E., soft and no good, and if there was anything her short life had taught her, it was that a person must be tough. Otherwise, you were had.

And Galadriel Hopkins was not ready to be had. But she must hurry. It didn't matter whether the people who hovered over her had fat laps or computer brains. For if a person could crack under heat or cold, a combination of the two seemed guaranteed to do in even the gutsy Galadriel.

By now she would have preferred to get Mr Randolph's money on her own and leave both William Ernest and Agnes Stokes out of it, but in her haste she acted stupidly and used them both.

The opportunity fell into her lap unexpectedly. Trotter had never asked her to baby-sit with William Ernest before, but suddenly two days after the card joke bombed, Trotter announced that she was taking Mr Randolph to pick up a few things at the dime store and would Gilly watch William Ernest while they were gone.

It was too perfect. She should have realized that, but her anxiety to get the money and get going had fuzzed her common sense. With shaking hands, she leafed through the fat suburban phone book until she found the number for the Stokeses in Thompson Park who supposedly lived on Aspen Avenue. (Another of the world's lies. The senior Stokeses had long before left the Washington area, abandoning Agnes to a maternal grandmother, seventy-five years old, by the name of Gertrude Berkheimer. But Agnes's delinquent father was still listed in the directory just as though he had never left her.)

Agnes arrived immediately, nearly falling over herself with joy that Gilly had not only invited her over but was actually asking for her help in carrying out a secret and obviously illegal plot. She agreed, without objection, to being the lookout at Mr Randolph's house, although Gilly suspected she would have preferred an inside role. Agnes was to do her whistle, which she claimed could be heard a mile away, should the taxi bearing Trotter and Mr Randolph return while Gilly was still inside.

Prying W.E. away from the TV and explaining his part to him proved far more difficult.

'I don't understand,' he said for what seemed to be the thirtieth time, blinking stupidly behind his glasses.

Gilly started all over again from the beginning as patiently as she could.

'Mr Randolph wants you and me to do him a favour. He's got something on the top shelf in his living room that he needs, and he can't see to get it down. I told him you and me weren't too busy this afternoon, so he says, "Miss Gilly, could you and William Ernest, who is just like a grandson to me, do me a tremendous favour while I am busy at the store?" So of course I told him we'd be glad to help out. You being just like a grandson to him and all.' She paused.

'What kind of favour?'

'Just get this stuff down off the shelf for him.'

'Oh.' Then, 'What stuff?'

'William Ernest. I haven't got all day. Do you want to help or not?'

He guessed so. Well, it would have to do. They had already delayed far too long. She gave Agnes some last-minute instructions out of range of the boy's earshot. Agnes would have to be paid in cold cash to keep her big mouth you-know-what. Then she went and got W.E. by the hand, and using the key that Trotter kept, they let themselves into Mr Randolph's house.

The house was dark and damp-feeling even in the daytime, but fortunately the boy was used to it and walked right in.

Gilly pointed out the top shelf of the bookcase. 'He told me he had the stuff right behind that big red book.'

W.E. looked up.

'See which one I'm talking about?'

He nodded, then shook his head. 'I can't reach it.'

'Of course not, stu – I can't reach it, either. That's why we both have to do it.'

'Oh.'

'Now look. I'm going to push this big blue chair over and stand on the arm. Then I want you to climb up the back of the chair and get on my shoulders...'

He drew back. 'I want to wait for Trotter.'

'We can't do that, William Ernest, honey. You know how hard it is on Trotter climbing up and down. It wouldn't be good for her.' He was still hesitant. 'Besides, I think it's kind of a surprise for Trotter. Mr Randolph doesn't want her to know about it. Yet.'

The boy came close to the chair and tiptoed up toward her. 'I'm scared,' he whispered.

'Sure you are. But just think, man, how proud everybody's going to be later. After the surprise can be told and everything. When they find out who it was that...'

He was already climbing up on the chair. It was an old, solid overstuffed one, so that when he stood on the arm and then on the back, it never moved. Gilly got up on the chair's fat arm and helped him onto her shoulders and held his legs. The little cuss was heavier than he looked.

'OK. First pull out that big red book I showed you.'

He grabbed her hair with his left hand and stretched toward the shelf without straightening and pulled out the book. It fell to the floor with a crash.

'I dropped it.'

'Don't worry about it! Just look back there behind where it was.'

He leaned forward. Ouch – she was afraid he'd take her hair out like weeds from a wet garden.

'It's dark.'

'Look, man! No, stick your hand up in there.'

She had to shift her balance as he leaned forward to keep from crashing to the floor herself.

'*Pow*,' he said softly, bringing back a dusty fist. In it was a rubber-banded roll of bills.

Gilly reached up.

'Don't let go my legs!' He dropped the money and grabbed her hair with both hands.

'Is there any more?'

'*Wheeeeeeeeet!*' Agnes's signal.

Gilly nearly fell off the chair as she snatched W.E. off her shoulders, then scrambled back on the top of the chairback, tilted 'Sarsaparilla to Sorcery' back in place, jumped down, stuffed the roll of bills into her jeans, shoved the heavy chair forward, grabbed a startled William, and dragged him out the back door.

'I gotta give it to Mr Randolph later, when Trotter isn't around,' she explained to the blinking owl eyes. 'Look I gotta go to the bathroom. You go help Trotter get Mr Randolph into the house. Oh – and tell Agnes to go home. I'll see her tomorrow.'

But Agnes was waiting for her in Trotter's hallway,

lounging against the stairs. 'Find what you was looking for?'

'No luck.'

Agnes looked down at Gilly's jeans. 'Then what's bulging your pocket?'

'OK. I found some, but I didn't find much.'

'How much did you find?'

'Hell, Agnes, I don't know.'

'I'll help you count.'

'I swear, Agnes, I'll help you rearrange your nose if you don't get out of here. I promised I'd give you something for helping, and I will, but I can't now, and if you don't understand that, you're in worse shape than I thought.'

Agnes stuck out her bottom lip. 'If it wasn't for me, you'd be caught right now.'

'I know, Agnes, and I won't forget that. But if you hang around now, we'll both be caught. So get out, and keep your mouth shut.'

Without waiting for further sulks, Gilly pushed past Agnes and ran up the staircase. She shut her door and pulled the bureau in front of it. Then she took out the special drawer and began to tape the money to the bottom with a sinking heart. Thirty-four dollars. Thirty-four measly dollars. Forty-four, counting the ten she had already. It had seemed like more in William's fist and bulging in her jeans. She counted it again to make sure. No, there was no more. Five five-dollar bills and nine ones. It had seemed like more because of all the singles. She laid out a one to give to Agnes, then reluctantly swapped it for a five. Agnes would not be bought off cheaply, she knew. If only she had done it by herself. It cost too much to use people. Why had she thought she couldn't do it alone? She had been in too big a hurry. She should have taken more time, and planned more carefully. Now she had gotten both Agnes and W.E. involved and all for a measly forty-four – no, thirty-nine – dollars. Then remembering the weight of W.E. on her neck and shoulders and the pain as he yanked her hair in terror, she started to count out another dollar, but that would leave her only thirty-eight. It would take a lot more to get even as far as the Mississippi River. She returned W.E.'s dollar to the stack.

She would have to search again, but she would go back by herself the next time. As soon as she figured out a plan.

Dust. The thought hit her after supper when they were all sitting in the living room watching the evening news. Suddenly she saw it, lying like a grey frost upon the TV set. Dust! She would go on a campaign, dusting first this house and then the other. She jumped to her feet.

'Trotter!'

Slowly Trotter shifted her attention from Walter Cronkite to Gilly. 'Yeah, honey?'

'Mind if I dust in here?'

'Dust?' Trotter spoke the word as though it were the name of an exotic and slightly dangerous game. 'I guess not.' Her gaze slid back toward the screen. 'Whyn't you wait till we're through watching TV, though?'

Gilly jiggled her foot through a Central American earthquake and the bribery trial of a congressman from who cared where.

She couldn't stand waiting. She ran into the kitchen. She now knew how she could get the money on her own and every minute seemed to matter. Under the sink were some old rags – and could you believe it? – a quarter bottle of furniture polish. She poured some on one of the rags which she had carefully dampened just as Mrs Nevins always did and proceeded to clean the never-used dining room with its dark, heavy table and six chairs.

One side of the rag was black in two swipes, but Gilly turned it over and poured out more polish. The steady wiping and polishing with the 'clean, dry cloth' fell into a rhythm that began to calm her inner frenzy. By the time she got to the picture over the buffet, she not only cleaned out the niches of the carved frame but she hunted up Windex and paper towels to wash the faces and so forths of the baby angels who were tripping around on clouds with only a ribbon or a stray wing to cover their private parts (as Mrs Nevins used to call them).

Meantime in the living room, the volume of Trotter's voice told Gilly that Walter Cronkite had called it a day, but she no longer needed to rush. Gently she wiped off the last streak of Windex.

By supper the next night she had finished cleaning everything but the living-room chandelier. And how could one do that without a stepladder?

'Oh, forget it, Gilly, honey. The place looks beautiful. No one's going to notice the chandelier,' said Trotter.

'I will,' said Gilly. 'I gotta have a tall stool or a stepladder or something. Then I could do the top kitchen cabinets, too.'

'Mercy. Next thing I know you'll be wiping me right out with all the rest of the trash.'

William Ernest looked up from his meat loaf in alarm.

Mr Randolph was chuckling. 'There is no danger of that, Mrs Trotter.'

'Well, you know what the Good Book says, Dust to dust ...'

'No!' squeaked William Ernest. 'You ain't dusty!'

'Oh, bless you, sweetheart. I was only talking crazy.'

'Nobody will take away William Ernest's Mrs Trotter; now, will they, Miss Gilly?' Mr Randolph reached out and felt for the boy's head and patted it.

'Of course not,' said Gilly sharply. 'I just want something to stand on to finish my job.'

'My, my,' said Mr Randolph, 'You really have yourself a prize helper here, Mrs Trotter. Young people nowadays hardly ...'

'If you want, Mr Randolph...' She would have to be careful – talk slowly as though the idea were just occurring to her – 'I could maybe do your house when I finish here. Course I'd have to have a stepladder, probably –'

'Didn't I say she was a prize, Mrs Trotter?' Mr Randolph was beaming. 'I might even have a ladder in my basement...'

Gilly jumped up from the table, then caught herself – slow down, slow down. Her heart was pumping crazily. She made herself sit down.

'Maybe after supper I could take a look. I'd sure like to finish that chandelier tonight.'

Trotter and Mr Randolph nodded and chuckled happily. People were so dumb sometimes you almost felt bad to take advantage of them – but not too bad. Not when it was your only way to get where you had to go.

The stepladder was old and rickety, but it would beat trying to climb those bookshelves of Mr Randolph's, which looked as though they might come right over on top of you if you pulled at them. She set the ladder up under Trotter's chandelier, and as she painstakingly wiped each piece of glass with her ammonia-water rag, she would have to grab the ladder from time to time, dizzy as she was with the smell of the ammonia and the thought that by tomorrow night at this time she'd be on her way to California.

Late that night she packed the brown bag and shoved it far under the bed. Tomorrow from the school pay phone, she'd call the bus station and find out how much the ticket cost. Then all she had to do was get the rest of the money.

Gilly was coming out of the phone booth the next day when Agnes appeared demanding her money. She pretended to be grumpy about the five dollars Gilly gave her, but there was a greedy gleam in her eyes. She was pleased, all right.

'Can we get more?' she asked.

Gilly shook her head. 'That's all there was. I split it three ways.'

'Looked like a lot in your pocket yesterday.'

'Yeah, but the rest was all in ones.'

'I don't see why you split equal with that weird kid. He wouldn't know the difference.'

'He's not as dumb as he looks.' Gilly looked Agnes straight in the eyes. 'He acts stupid, maybe, but if he thought you and me were cheating on him...'

Agnes shrugged. 'Well,' she said, 'next time, let's not use him.'

'OK, sure, next time,' Gilly agreed, knowing happily that there would be no next time with creepy Agnes the Stoke. Tonight she would be bound for her new life – her real life.

She got rid of Agnes at the front gate with some lie about Trotter forcing her to scrub all the dirty pots in the house. Agnes said she'd go on home. She wasn't too crazy about cleaning pots and pans.

The stepladder was in the hall. Gilly put her schoolbooks down on the table and went right to it. As she was leaning to pick it up – 'Gilly, honey, want some snack?'

She straightened up quickly. It would be better to eat while she had the chance. She gave the ladder a pat and went into the kitchen.

Trotter was sitting at the table. She seemed to have finished her daily Bible reading, for the Good Book, still open, was pushed to one side. Right before her was a piece of notebook paper, half filled with her square, laborious script. She had a nineteen-cent ball-point clutched tightly in her right hand. When Gilly came in, the huge woman smiled shyly at her over the top of her reading glasses.

'Writing one of my old children. I do miss 'em when they grow up and leave me, but the Good Lord knows I ain't much at writing.' She looked down at her letter and sighed. 'There's more of them cookies in the tin box next to the refrigerator.'

Gilly poured herself a twelve-ounce glass of milk and took four of the cookies.

'Sit down, Gilly, honey. I ain't really busy.'

Gilly sat down at the far side of the table.

'Things is going better for you now, ain't they, honey?'

'OK.'

'I been meaning to say to you how much I appreciate the way you've been making friends with William Ernest.'

'Yeah, OK.'

'Like Miz Ellis says, you're a special kind of person, Gilly. It makes me praise the Lord to see you so busy helping 'stead of hurting.'

Shut up, Trotter.

'You got so much to give. Mercy, what most of us wouldn't give for half your brains.'

Shut up, Trotter, shut up!

The silent commands were obeyed because just then William Ernest, honey, appeared, and Trotter roused her great hulk from the table to get him his snack.

Trotter, baby, if you had half my brains you'd know to let the boy do things for himself. If I were going to stay here, I'd teach him how. You want to so hard, and you don't know how. Even the birds know to shove the babies out of the nest. If I were going to be here, I'd make a man of your little marshmallow. But I can't stay. I might go soft and stupid, too. Like I did at the Dixons'. I let her fool me with all that rocking and love talk. I called her Mama and crawled up on her lap when I had to cry. My god! She said I was her own little baby, but when they moved to Florida, I was put out like the rest of the trash they left behind. I can't go soft – not as long as I'm nobody's real kid – not while I'm just something to play musical chairs with . . .

An elbow pierced her rib cage.

Gilly jerked awake. What the hell? W.E. was trying to attract her attention without getting Trotter's, mouthing some words through a full load of cookie crumbs.

Huh? She asked the question by raising her eyebrows.

He swallowed. Then 'Surprise,' he mouthed, pointing his head in Trotter's general direction.

She took her head with exaggerated vigour. 'Not yet!' she mouthed back. 'Later.'

A little grin escaped and danced around his face.

Gilly sighed. If she didn't watch herself, she'd start liking the little jerk. She excused herself. 'I'm going to get on to my dusting over at Mr Randolph's.'

W.E. made as if to follow.

'Naw, William Ernest. You better watch *Sesame Street* today. I'm going to help you with your reading later on, and you have to be real sharp. Right, Trotter?'

'You better believe it.'

She knocked several times at Mr Randolph's door before he opened it, his tie and shirt awry and his face still clogged with sleep.

'I – uh – brought your stepladder back, Mr Randolph.'

'Oh? Oh, thank you, thank you. Just put it down out there on the porch.'

'But – but – I thought since I was here and had the ladder and all, I might come on in and – uh – start to work.'

'Oh, Miss Gilly. You don't have to worry. I was just talking the other night. What I can't see isn't likely to hurt me.'

'I don't mind. I want to help.'

'Every week or so my son over in Virginia comes and brings a lady to vacuum a little. It's really all I need.'

'But I want to' – god – 'What I mean is, I want to help Mrs Trotter, and you know how she is, she really doesn't need my help. But I figured if I do something for you, it will be like doing something for her...'

'Bless you, you sweet little lady. How can I say No to that?'

It worked. He stepped aside for her to come in and shuffled along right behind her into the living room. Was he going to stay in there, his sightless eyes following the sound of her?

'Why don't you just go up and finish your nap, Mr Randolph? I feel bad waking you up like this.'

He chuckled and stretched out in the worn blue plush armchair, his feet up on the equally worn stool. He closed his eyes.

'Wouldn't you rest better up on your bed or something? I'm – I'm going to be working in here. Making a lot of noise.'

'Mercy, Miss Gilly, I can rest in heaven. In the meantime, it is human company that I treasure. It won't bother you if I just sit here, will it? I promise not to make suggestions.'

'Why don't I come back later? I don't want to bother you.'

'Bother me? I'm delighted.'

She kept her eyes on the little man as she carefully set up the stepladder at the far end of the bookcase wall. The blue plush chair was exactly where she'd shoved it two days earlier, catercornered three feet from the place she'd have to set up the ladder in order to reach 'Sarsaparilla to Sorcery'.

'Excuse me, Mr Randolph.' Her voice barely squeaked out. She cleared her throat. 'Mr Randolph!' Now she was yelling. 'I'm going to have to move your chair.'

He got up like an obedient child. Gilly shoved and pushed and tugged the heavy chair to a place opposite the red encyclopedia. She arranged the chair and then the stool, and then took Mr Randolph's elbow and led him to them.

'Now your chair's just opposite from where it was before.'

'I hope you haven't strained yourself, Miss Gilly.'

'Right between the end of the couch and the corner of the desk. Couple of feet on either side, OK?'

'Fine, fine.' He sat down and stretched out again.

Gilly went back to the stepladder, climbed the first step, and then backed down.

'I guess I'll begin with the windows over the desk.'

He smiled his funny little blank-eyed smile. 'You're the doctor, Miss Gilly.'

She did the windows and the desk, then moved the ladder around Mr Randolph to the smaller of the two giant bookcases. She went back and dusted the picture over the couch, which was of fancily dressed white people in another century having an elaborate picnic in a woods. She kept looking over her shoulder at Mr Randolph, who lay motionless with his eyes closed. Since he'd been known to sleep on Trotter's couch with his eyes wide open, there was no way under heaven to tell if he were wide awake or dead asleep. But he wasn't snoring. That was worrisome.

But, hell. The man was blind and half deaf. Why should it matter in the least that he was sitting right there in the room while she robbed him of money he was too old to remember having? Still – the closer she got to 'Sarsaparilla' the more her heart carried on like the entire percussion section of a marching band doing 'The Stars and Stripes Forever'.

At last she moved the stepladder directly in front of the place and took a step up, glancing sideways at Mr Randolph. He didn't move. She eased up the ladder trying not to make noise, but it creaked and swayed under her weight. From the next to the top step she could reach 'Sar-

saparilla to Sorcery' without stretching. She braced her left
leg hard against the cold metal of the ladder, took out the
now familiar volume, and laid it gently on the ladder top.

Nothing was visible except dust. She took out books on
either side, dusting each one with a kind of fury. Still
nothing.

Mr Randolph was shifting in his chair across the room.
She looked into his blank white eyes. Oh, god. Maybe he
could really see. Maybe it was all a trick to fool people.
She froze.

'You certainly are doing a beautiful job. So careful. My,
my, I don't know when this room has been so thoroughly
cleaned before.'

'I – I – I'm sort of straightening up the book shelves.'

'Fine, fine.' He was bobbing his head. 'Now if there
were just some way you could straighten up this old brain
of mine as well...'

She was not going to panic. He couldn't see. Of course,
he couldn't see. It was really better that he was in the
room. Nobody would suspect her of stealing right from
under his nose. She dusted the space and then moved 'Sarsaparilla' down to the shelf that held the rest of the encyclopedia set. On the shelf from which it had come, she proceeded to remove, one by one, all the other books, wiping
carefully behind each one to the dark-stained wood at the
back of the case. With every book her hope rose and fell,
rising a little less and falling a little more each time. At
last she knew that her lie to Agnes had proved all too true.
There was no more money.

Fear and anticipation curdled in her stomach. She
wanted to throw up.

Mr Randolph was chatting away happily. She couldn't
seem to tune in the words, just the maddeningly cheerful
tone of his high-pitched voice. She wanted to throw a book
at the noise – kick over the stepladder – crash a chair

through the window – at the very least scream out her frustration.

But, of course, she didn't. Wrapped in a silent, frozen rage, she folded the stepladder and carried it to the basement.

'You going now, Miss Gilly?' The voice followed her down and up the steps and out of the house. 'Thank you, thank you. Come back for another little visit, won't you? Be sure to tell Mrs Trotter what a lovely help you've been.'

She made no attempt to answer him. It didn't matter what he thought. He was of no use to her. Thirty-nine stinking dollars.

She went straight to her room, took the brown suitcase from under the bed, and unpacked it. Then she ripped out a sheet of paper through the rings of her notebook, lay down on the bed, and pressing on her math book wrote:

> 1408 Aspen Ave.
> Thompson Park, Md.

Dear Courtney Rutherford Hopkins,

I received your card. I am sorry to bother you with my problems, but as my real mother, I feel you have a right to know about your daughter's situation.

At the present time, it is very desperate, or I would not bother you. The foster mother is a religious fanatic. Besides that she can hardly read and write and has a very dirty house and weird friends.

She started to write 'coloured' but erased it, not sure how Courtney might react.

There is another kid here who is probably mentally retarded.

I am expected to do most of the work including taking care of him (the mentally retarded boy) which is very hard with all my school-work, too.

I have saved up $39 toward my ticket to California. Please send me the rest at your earliest convenience.

She wrote 'Love' then changed it to:

> Yours sincerely,
> your daughter,
> Galadriel Hopkins

P.S. I am very smart and can take care of myself, so I will not be a burden to you in any way.

P.S. Again. I have checked the cost of a bus ticket to San Francisco. It is exactly $136.60 one way. I will get a job and pay you back as soon as possible.

She listened at the top of the stairs until she heard Trotter go into the downstairs bathroom. Then she crept into the kitchen, stole an envelope and a stamp from the kitchen drawer, and ran to the corner to mail her letter before the rage could defrost and change her mind.

# The One-Way Ticket

Not everything in the letter to Courtney had been absolutely true, but surely the part about Trotter being a religious fanatic was. She read the Bible and prayed every day, always joining Mr Randolph's grace over the food. Besides, anybody who started for church at nine in the morning on Sunday and didn't get home until after twelve thirty had to be peculiar.

Sunday mornings were torture to Gilly. The church was a strange little white frame building stuck up on a hill behind the police station, built when the city was a country town instead of part of the metropolitan Washington sprawl. The church didn't fit in the modern world anymore than the people who went there did.

The children's Sunday-school class, in which both Gilly and W.E. were lumped with the five other six- to twelve-year-olds in the church, was presided over by an ancient Miss Minnie Applegate, who reminded her seven charges every Sunday that she had been 'saved' by Billy Sunday. Who in the hell was Billy Sunday? He sounded like a character from the comics. Billy Sunday meet Brenda Starr. Also, Miss Applegate neglected to say what Billy Sunday had saved her from. A burning building? The path of a speeding locomotive? Or indeed, having been so luckily preserved, what good had her pickling accomplished for either herself or the world?

Old Applegate would do things like lecture them on the Ten Commandments and then steadfastly refuse to explain what adultery was.

'But, Miss Applegate,' an eight-year-old had sensibly asked, 'if we don't know what adultery is, how can we know if we're doing it or not?'

Gilly, of course, knew all about adultery. In whispered conversations between Sunday school and church, she offered for sale not only the definition of the word but some juicy neighbourhood examples (which had lately come to her attention, thanks to Agnes Stokes). In this way she gained seventy-eight cents in coins previously designated for the church collection plate.

The preacher was as young as the Sunday-school teacher was old. He, too, was high on getting saved and other matters of eternal preservation. But his grammar was worse than Trotter's, and, to Gilly's disgust, he'd stumble over words of more than one syllable whenever he read the Bible. Nobody but a religious fanatic would put up with such gross ignorance for over an hour every week of their lives – nobody but religious fanatics and the innocent victims they forced to go to church.

Unlike some of the women, Trotter didn't carry on over the preacher at the church door, which made Gilly bold enough to ask her once, 'How can you stand him?' It was the wrong question. Trotter sucked in her breath and glowered down at her like Moses at the Israelites' golden calf. 'Who am I,' she thundered, 'to pass judgement on the Lord's anointed?' Would anybody but a fanatic say a thing like that?

Mr Randolph went to the black Baptist church. The same taxi that took Trotter and the children to the white Baptist church dropped him off on the way and picked him up on the way home. Gilly noted that the black Baptists dressed fancier and smiled more than the whites. But their services lasted even longer, and often W.E. would have to run in and get the old man out of his service while the taxi meter impatiently ticked away. It was usually past two by the time they got out of their Sunday clothes, cooked dinner, and finally sat down to their long, lazy meal.

The Sunday after the futile dusting, Mr Randolph surprised everyone by refusing seconds.

'Oh, you must know, Mrs Trotter, how it pains me to say No to this exquisite chicken, but my son is coming over about three.'

At the word 'son', something clanked inside Gilly's chest. Suppose the son noticed that something was funny in Mr Randolph's living room? The chair on the opposite side, the books rearranged? Suppose he knew where the money should have been?

'Oh, you got time for a piece of pie, now, don't you, Mr Randolph? It's cherry today.'

'Cherry. My, my.' Mr Randolph held his bony thumb and index finger an inch apart. 'About so much, all right? I'm helpless before your cherry pies, Mrs Trotter. Totally helpless.'

He was chewing the pie blissfully when suddenly he stopped. 'Oh, my. Have I got spots on my clothes? My son gets so upset.'

Trotter put her fork down and studied him. 'You look good, Mr Randolph. Only just a little something on your tie.'

'Oh, mercy, mercy. The boy is always looking for some excuse to say I can't take care of myself so he can drag me over to his big house in Virginia.' He dipped his napkin into his water glass and tried to dab his tie, completely missing the offending spots.

'Oh, shoot, Mr Randolph. Let me get you one of Melvin's old ties to wear. I don't know why I still got so much of his stuff around anyhow.' She sniffed as if to clear away a memory of the late Mr Trotter. 'Gilly, run up to my room and look in the back of the closet, will you? There's a dozen or more on a coat hanger.' Before Gilly got out the

door, she added, 'Just pick a nice one, hear? Not one of the
real loud ones.' She turned, half apologetically to Mr Randolph. 'Sometimes in those last years, if Melvin was feeling
low, he'd go out and buy some wild tie and wear it every
day for a week.' She shook her head. 'I guess I should
praise the Lord it wasn't some wild woman he was hanging round his neck.'

Mr Randolph giggled. 'Why don't you bring me a wild
one, Miss Gilly? I need to wake up that fifty-year-old
senior citizen I've got for a son.'

Trotter threw back her massive head and belly-laughed.
'You're some kinda man, Mr Randolph.'

'Well, you're some kind of lady.'

Gilly fled up the stairs. These scenes between Trotter
and Mr Randolph made her insides curl. It was weird to
see old people carry on, old people who weren't even the
same colour.

But it was not that silly little flirtation that was bother-
ing her. It was a vision of Mr Randolph's prissy fifty-year-
old son poking around his father's living room. So when
she saw Trotter's purse with its no-good fastener lying
wide open on the bed, inviting her, practically demanding
her to look in, she did so. Good god. Trotter must have
just cashed her check from county welfare. Gilly did a
quick count – at least a hundred. Another hundred would
get her all the way to California – all the way to Courtney
Rutherford Hopkins, all the way home.

She stuffed the money in her pocket, went to the closet,
and found the hanger full of Melvin's madness. She chose
the gaudiest one there – four-inch-high ballet dancers in
purple tutus, their pink legs pirouetting on a greenish four-
in-hand. She tiptoed to her own room, slipped the fat wad
of bills in her drawer under her T-shirts, and tiptoed back
to Trotter's door; once there, she slammed her feet down
and noisily descended the stairs.

'Oh, my sweet baby, what have you done?'

Gilly's blood went cold. How could Trotter know?

'That tie. It's the worst crime Melvin ever committed. Rest his precious soul.'

'Oh, good, good.' Mr Randolph was standing up, rubbing his wrinkled hands together in excitement. 'Tell me about it.'

'You better not take this one, Mr Randolph. It's got all these fat women jumping around.'

'Really?' The little brown face beamed. 'Are they decent?'

'Well, they ain't naked, but they might as well be. Little purple flimflams –'

'Tutus,' prompted Gilly primly, gratefully recovering from her earlier shock.

'What?' asked Trotter.

'Tutus. They're wearing tutus.'

Trotter roared. 'Ain't that perfect? Too-toos. Too-too skimpy for words.'

Mr Randolph was already taking off his spotted black tie to make room for Melvin's dancing ladies.

'You sure now, Mr Randolph? I don't want your son thinking I'm some kinda wicked influence on his good Baptist father.'

Gilly began to wonder if poor Mr Randolph was going to choke on his own giggles. 'He doesn't ever need to know where the tie came from. I give you my solemn word' – this from a man hysterical with laughter. Jeez.

Trotter knotted the tie for him with the kind of assured expertise born of knotting one man's tie for more than a quarter of a century. She stepped back to appraise the effect.

'Well – what do you think, Gilly, honey? That do something for Mr Randolph?'

'It's OK.'

'OK? We gotta do better than that! How 'bout you, William Ernest, honey? How do you like Mr Randolph's new tie?'

'It's beautiful,' the boy whispered reverently.

'See, well.' Trotter was immediately sober. 'William Ernest approves.'

'Good, good,' said Mr Randolph, his dignity also once again intact. 'Would you walk with me back to my house then, son?'

The boy slid out of his chair and took the old man's hand.

'See you tomorrow, hear?' Trotter said.

'Thank you. Yes. Thank you. And you, too, Miss Gilly. See you tomorrow.'

'Yeah. OK,' said Gilly, though by this time tomorrow she figured to be in Missouri at the very least.

She dried the dishes as Trotter washed them and put them to drain, her mind aboard the Greyhound bus skimming across something that looked like a three-dimensional version of the topographical map in her geography book.

Trotter beside her was chuckling again over Mr Randolph's sporting Melvin's dancing ladies. 'His son's this big lawyer' – lawyer! – 'over in Virginia. I'd give a pretty penny to see his face when he gets a load of that tie. Mercy on us, wouldn't I ever?'

After they finished cleaning up in the kitchen, Trotter went into the living room and stretched out on the couch. Her one trip upstairs on Sundays was to change out of her good dress, so she'd be on the couch the rest of the day, napping or laboriously reading the Sunday paper. W.E., back from next door, turned on the TV and lay down on the rug to watch an old movie.

Now was the time. Gilly started for the stairs.

'You want to join us, honey? There's a football game on Channel 9, 'less W.E. cares about this movie.'

W.E got up, obediently ready to switch channels.

'No,' Gilly said. 'Not right now. I got things to do.'

'Well, OK, honey.'

If she was going to go, she would have to leave now. By tonight Trotter would go upstairs and find the money gone, and nothing was sure about what might happen with Mr Randolph's lawyer son next door.

She packed quickly although her hands shook. The first thing was to gather all the money together and put it into her pocket. It made a lump as big as an orange. Too bad she'd thrown away that silly shoulder bag Mrs Nevins had bought her last Christmas.

Her jacket – 'First thing next week we're going to have to buy you a good, warm coat,' Trotter had said. She had been waiting for the support check – her jacket was hanging by the front door, downstairs, past the open living-room door. Trotter was probably asleep, and, if Gilly was very quiet, perhaps W.E. wouldn't hear.

She crept down, keeping her suitcase under her right arm to conceal it as best she could with her body. Crossing the short, bright strip before the door, she glanced in. Neither head turned. She was safely to the front door. She took her jacket off the hook and poked it above the suitcase, so that she had a free hand for the knob.

'Where you going?' She jumped around at W.E.'s whisper. In the dark hallway his glasses flashed.

'Just out,' she whispered back. Oh, god, make him shut up.

He did shut up and stood silently, looking first at her, then at the suitcase, then back at her.

'Don't go.' His little face squeezed up at her like his tiny voice.

'I got to,' she said through her teeth. Opening the door, pulling it shut behind her, shifting the suitcase and jacket to either hand, and running, running, running, down the hill, the pulse in her forehead pounding as hard as her sneakered feet pounded the sidewalk.

Once around the corner, she slowed down. Someone might notice her if they saw her running. No bus came by. There were hardly any on Sundays. She settled herself at once to walk the mile or so to the bus station, stopping to put on her thin jacket against the November wind. The bus would be heated, she reminded herself, and in California the sun always shines.

It was dusk by the time she got to the bus station. She went straight to the ladies' room and combed her hair and tucked her shirt into her jeans. She tried to tell herself that she looked much older than eleven. She was tall, but totally bustless. Hell. She zipped up her jacket, stood up straight, and went out to the ticket counter.

The man didn't even look up.

'I want a ticket to California, please.' As soon as the words were out, she heard her mistake.

'California where?' He glanced up now, looking at her through half-open lids.

'Uh – San Francisco. San Francisco, California.'

'One way or round trip?'

Whatever happened to Lady Cool? 'One – one way.'

He punched some buttons and a ticket magically emerged. 'One thirty-six sixty including tax.'

She had it. She had enough. With trembling hands, she took the wad of bills from her pocket and began to count it out.

The man watched lazily. 'Your mother know where you are, kid?'

Come on, Gilly. You can't fall apart now. She pulled herself straight and directed into his sleepy eyes the look she usually reserved for teachers and principals. 'I'm going to see my mother. She lives in San Francisco.'

'OK,' he said, taking her money and recounting it before he handed her the ticket. 'Bus leaves at eight thirty.'

'Eight thirty?'

'Yeah. Want to check your bag?'

'It's only four-thirty now.'

'That's right.'

'That's four hours from now.'

'Right again.'

'But I want to leave as soon as I can.'

'Look, kid, you came in here and asked me for a ticket. I gave you one on the next bus.' He sighed. 'OK,' he said and consulted his book. 'You can take the five o'clock into Washington and catch a six twenty-two out of there.' He stuck out his hand. 'I'll have to fix you another ticket.'

She gave it back.

'It'll take me a while,' he said. 'I gotta check the routing.' He nodded to the seats across the waiting room. 'Just sit down over there. I'll call you.'

She hesitated, then reluctantly obeyed. She didn't like the idea of leaving both the money and the ticket there, but she was afraid he'd ask more questions if she protested.

He was a long time at it. He was on the phone a while, talking in a muffled voice. Then he was poring through his books. Once he got up and went back into the baggage room and stayed away for several minutes.

It was almost four forty-five. If he didn't hurry, she might miss the five o'clock bus. She got up and got a drink from the water cooler. The water was warm, and somebody had dropped a piece of gum on the drain. She went back to the red plastic seat still thirsty.

The clock said four forty-eight when the clerk came back and sat down without even looking her way.

'My ticket?'

But just then a man and woman came in, and the clerk got busy with them. It wasn't fair. She'd been there waiting since four thirty. Gilly stood up and started for the counter. She didn't even see the policeman until she felt his hands on her arm.

Gilly snatched her arm back as she looked to see who had touched her.

'Where you headed, little girl?' He spoke quietly as though not to disturb anyone.

'To see my mother,' said Gilly tightly. Oh, god, make him go away.

'All the way to San Francisco by yourself?' She knew then the clerk had called him. Damn!

'Yes.'

'I see,' he said with a quick look at the clerk, who was now staring at them with both eyes well open.

'I haven't done anything wrong.'

'Nobody's charging you with anything.' The policeman pulled his cap straight and said in a very careful, very patient voice, 'Who you been staying with here in the area?'

She didn't have to answer him. It was none of his business.

'Look. Somebody's going to be worried about you.'

Like hell.

He cleared his throat. 'What about giving me your telephone number? So I can just check things out?'

She glared at him.

He coughed and cleared his throat again and looked up at the clerk. She might have gotten away in that instant – except for the money. Where could she go without the money? 'I think,' the policeman was saying, 'I'd better take her in for a little talk.'

The clerk nodded. He seemed to be enjoying himself.

'Here's the money she brought in.' He held up a manila envelope. The policeman took her gently by the arm and walked her to the counter. The clerk handed him the envelope.

'That's my money,' Gilly protested.

'I'll just bet it is, kid,' the clerk said with a fake smile.

If she had known what to do, she would have done it. She tried to make her brain tell her, but it lay frozen in her skull like a woolly mammoth deep in a glacier. All the way to the station she asked it, Shall I jump out of the car at the next light and run? Should I just forget about the damn money? But the woolly mammoth slept on, refusing to stir a limb in her behalf.

In a back room behind the police station's long counter two policemen tried to question her. The new one, a big blond, was asking the first one: 'She ain't got no ID?'

'Well, I'm not going to search her, and Judy's gone out to get her supper.'

'What about the suitcase?'

'Yeah, better check through there.'

She wanted to yell at them to leave her stuff alone, but she couldn't break through the ice.

The blond policeman riffled carelessly through her clothes. He found Courtney's picture almost at once. 'This your mother, kid?'

'Put that down,' she whispered.

'Oh, now she's talking.'

'She said to put her picture down, Mitchell.'

'OK, OK. Just trying to do my job.' He put the picture down and continued to poke through the suitcase. 'Bingo,' he said, picking up the postcard. He read it carefully before handing it to the other officer. 'All here, Rhine. Name and current address. And big surprise! She does know somebody in San Francisco.'

The one called Rhine read the postcard and then came and stooped down beside her chair.

'Is this your father's address here?' he asked, pointing at the address on the card.

She sat perfectly still, staring him down.

Rhine shook his head, stood up, and handed the card back to Mitchell. 'Check out who lives at that address and give them a call, will you?'

Within a half hour, a red-faced Trotter, holding the hand of a white-faced William Ernest, puffed through the station-house door. Her eye immediately caught Gilly's, still seated in the room on the other side of the counter. She tried to smile, but Gilly jerked away from the gaze. The police-woman was back from her supper and on duty at the counter.

'Maime . . . Maime Trotter' – Trotter was puffing worse than if she'd run up her steps – 'Got a . . . taxi . . . waiting . . . No money . . . to . . . pay . . . him.'

'Just a minute, please.' Judy, the policewoman, came in and spoke quietly to Rhine, and then Rhine got up and they both went out to the counter. The only part of the conversation Gilly could make out was Trotter's breathy re-plies: 'Foster child . . . Yes – somewhere . . . San Francisco, yes, maybe so . . . County Social Services . . . Uh – Miz Miriam Ellis . . . yes . . . yes . . . no . . . no . . . no . . . Can some-one pay the taxicab? Still waiting out there . . .' Officer Rhine gave Trotter the yellow envelope. She sighed and nodded, taking out some money which she handed to him. He handed it to Mitchell, who handed it to the police-woman, who frowned but went out anyway to pay the cab driver.

'No, no,' Trotter was saying. 'Of course not. She's just a baby . . .' Trotter was still shaking her head at Rhine as he brought her back around the counter, W.E. clutching at her shabby coat.

Trotter's breath had returned, but her voice shook as she spoke to Gilly from the doorway. 'I come to take you home, Gilly, honey. Me and William Ernest come up to get you.'

Rhine came all the way in and stooped down again beside her. 'Mrs Trotter is not going to press charges. She wants you to come back.'

Press charges? Oh, the money. Did the stupid man think that Trotter would have her arrested? But how could she go back? Gilly the Great, who couldn't even run away? Botched the job. She stared at her fingers. The nails were grubby. She hated grubby fingernails.

'Gilly, honey . . .'

'Don't you want to go home?' Rhine was asking.

Want to go home? Don't I want to go home? Where in the hell do you think I was headed?

When she didn't answer him, Rhine stood up. 'Maybe we should keep her tonight and call Social Services in the morning.'

'You mean to lock the child up?'

'She'd be safe. It would just be overnight.'

'You don't think for one minute I'm going to let you lock a child of mine up in jail?'

'Maybe it would be best,' Rhine said quietly.

'Best? What do you mean? What are you trying to say?'

'She really doesn't seem to want to go with you, Mrs Trotter. Now, I don't know . . .'

'O, my dear Lord, you don't – O, my dear Lord –'

It was the closest to cursing Gilly had ever heard Trotter come to. She looked up into the fat, stricken face.

'O, my dear Lord. What can I do?'

'Gilly! Gilly!' William Ernest streaked across the room and began to beat his fists on her knees. 'Come home, Gilly. Please come home! Please, please!' The blood vessels stood out blue and strained on his white neck.

The ice in her frozen brain rumbled and cracked. She stood up and took his hand.

'Thank you, precious Jesus,' Trotter said.

Rhine cleared his throat. 'You don't have to go unless you want to. You know that, don't you?'

Gilly nodded. Trotter in the doorway lifted her arms, the brown purse dangling from one of them; the faulty clasp flew open as she did so. She dropped her arms, embarrassed, and forced the purse shut. 'I need another taxi, officer.'

'I'll get Mitchell to drive you,' he said.

# Pow

There was a fight between Trotter and Miss Ellis. Gilly heard the sounds of battle in the living room when she came in from school the next afternoon. 'Never, never, never!' Trotter was bellowing like an old cow deprived of its calf.

Gilly stopped still in the hallway, closing the door without a sound.

'Mrs Trotter, nobody at the agency looks at it as any indication of failure on your part –'

'You think I care what the agency thinks?'

'You're one of our most capable foster parents. You've been with us for more than twenty years. This won't affect your record with us. You're too valuable –'

'I don't give a spit about no record. You ain't taking Gilly.'

'We're trying to think of you –'

'No, you ain't. If you was thinking of me, you'd never come to me with such a fool notion.'

'This is a troubled child, Maime. She needs special –'

'No! I ain't giving her up. Never!'

'If you won't think of yourself, think of William Ernest. He's come too far in the last year to let – I've seen myself how she upsets him.'

'It was William Ernest got her to come home last night.' Trotter's voice was square and stubborn.

'Because he saw how upset *you* were. That doesn't mean she can't damage him.'

'William Ernest has lived with me for over two years. He's gonna make it. I know he is. Sometimes, Miz Ellis, you gotta walk on your heel and favour your toe even if it makes your heel a little sore.'

'I don't understand what you're driving at.'

'Somebody's got to favour Gilly for a little while. She's long overdue.'

'That's exactly it, Mrs Trotter. I'm quite aware of Gilly's needs. I've been her caseworker for nearly five years, and whether you believe it or not, I really care about her. But I don't think it's her needs we're talking about right now, is it?'

'What do you mean?'

'It's *your* needs.' Said very quietly.

A silence and then, 'Yes, Lord knows, I need her.' A funny broken sound like a sob came from Trotter. 'I like to die when I found her gone.'

'You can't do that, Mrs Trotter. You can't let them tear you to pieces.'

'Don't try to tell a mother how to feel.'

'You're a foster mother, Mrs Trotter.' Miss Ellis's voice was firm. 'You can't afford to forget that.'

Gilly's whole body was engulfed in a great aching. She opened and slammed the front door, pretending to have just come in. This time they heard her.

'That you, Gilly, honey?'

She went to the doorway of the living room. Both women were on their feet, flushed as though they'd been running a race.

'Well, Gilly,' Miss Ellis began, her voice glittering like a fake Christmas tree.

'Miz Ellis,' Trotter broke in loudly, 'was just saying how it's up to you.' There was a flash of alarm from the social worker which Trotter pretended not to see. 'You want to stay on here with William Ernest and me – that's fine.

You want her to find you someplace else – that's fine, too. You got to be the one to decide.' Her eyes shifted uneasily toward Miss Ellis.

'What about,' Gilly asked, her mouth going dry as a stale soda cracker, 'what about my real mother?'

Miss Ellis's eyebrows jumped. 'I wrote her, Gilly, several months ago, when we decided to move you from the Nevinses. She never answered.'

'She wrote me. She wants me to come out there.'

Miss Ellis looked at Trotter. 'Yes. I know about the postcard,' the caseworker said.

Those damned cops reading people's mail and blabbing, passing it around, snickering over it probably.

'Gilly. If – if she had really wanted you with her –'

'She does want me. She said so!'

'Then why hasn't she come to get you?' A hard edge had come into Miss Ellis's voice, and her eyebrows were twitching madly. 'It's been over eight years, Gilly. Even when she lived close by, she never came to see you.'

'It's different now!' – wasn't it? – 'She's gonna come! She really wants me!' – didn't she?

Trotter came over to her and laid her arm heavily on Gilly's shoulder. 'If she knowed you – if she just knowed what a girl she has – she'd be here in a minute.'

Oh, Trotter, don't be a fool. If she knew what I was like, she'd never come. It takes someone stupid like you – Gilly removed herself gently from under the weighty embrace and addressed herself to Miss Ellis, eye to eyebrow.

'Till she comes . . . till she comes for me, I guess I'll just stay here.'

Trotter wiped her face with her big hand and snuffled. 'Well, I'm sure we'll be seeing you sometime, Miz Ellis.'

The social worker wasn't going to be swept out quite so easily. She set her feet apart as though fearing Trotter might try to remove her bodily and said, 'Officer Rhine told me when he called that you had well over a hundred dollars with you last night.'

'Yeah?'

It came out sassy, but Miss Ellis just squinted her eyes and went on: 'It's hard to believe that it was all your money.'

'So?'

'So I call taking other people's money *stealing*, Miss Hopkins.'

'Yeah?'

Trotter patted Gilly's arm as if to shush her. 'So do we, Miz Ellis. Surely you don't think this is the first time something like this has happened to me over the last twenty years?'

'No, I know it's not.'

'Then how 'bout trusting me to handle it?'

Miss Ellis shook her head and smoothed her pants suit down over her rump before she put on her coat. 'I'll be in close touch,' she said.

Trotter nearly shoved her out the front door. 'We're going to do just fine. Don't worry your pretty little head about us, hear?'

'I get paid to worry, Mrs Trotter.'

Trotter smiled impatiently and closed the door quickly. When she turned back toward Gilly, her face was like Mount Rushmore stone.

Gilly blinked in surprise at the sudden and absolute change.

'I don't take lightly to stealing, you know.'

Gilly nodded. No use pretending sassiness.

'I figure that money ain't all mine, right?'

'No.'

'Well, where'd you get it?'

'I found it,' said Gilly softly.

Trotter came over and with two hands lifted Gilly's face to look into her own. 'Where did you get it, Gilly?'

'I found it behind some books next door.'

Trotter dropped her hands in disbelief. 'You stole from Mr Randolph?'

'It was just lying there behind the books. He probably didn't even –'

'Gilly, you stole it. Don't put no fancy name on it. It was his, and you took it, right?'

'I guess so.'

'How much?'

'Uh, for – thir –'

'Don't fool with me. How much?'

'Forty-four dollars,' Gilly said miserably.

'Well, you gotta take it back.'

'I can't.' Trotter stood there, hand on hip, staring at her until Gilly continued, 'I gave five dollars to Agnes Stokes.'

'You did, huh?'

Gilly nodded.

'Well' – a great sigh – 'I'll lend you the five to pay Mr Randolph back, and you can work it off.'

Giving back Mr Randolph's money was not as bad as it might have been. The old man apparently had no idea that there had been any money behind his books. Either he'd forgotten, or it had been put there by his wife, dead long before Trotter's Melvin. At any rate, when Gilly gave the forty-four dollars to him, Trotter looming behind her like a mighty army, he accepted her mumbled explanation without showing shock or undue curiosity, but with a strange litle dignity.

'Thank you,' he said, for once not doubling the phrase. He put the money in his pocket, rubbed his hands together briefly, and then put out his hand to be led to supper.

Gilly hesitated for a moment, waiting for the sermon

that was bound to pour forth, if not from him, surely from Trotter. But neither spoke, so she took Mr Randolph's hand, instead of his elbow as she usually did, as a kind of thank you.

Trotter had obviously never heard of either the minimum-wage or the child-labour laws. She posted the following sign in the kitchen:

| | |
|---|---|
| *Washing dishes and cleaning kitchen* | *10¢* |
| *Vacuuming downstairs* | *10¢* |
| *Cleaning both bathrooms including floors* | *10¢* |
| *Dusting* | *10¢* |
| *Helping William Ernest with schoolwork,* | |
| *one hour* | *25¢* |

Gilly began to spend a lot of time with W.E. She discovered several things. One was that the boy was not as dumb as he looked. If you held back and didn't press him, he could often figure out things for himself, but when you crowded him, he would choke right up, and if you laughed at him, he'd throw his hands up as if to protect his head from a blow. It finally occurred to Gilly that he really thought she would smack him every time he made a mistake.

Which was why, of course, Trotter tiptoed around the boy as though he would shatter at the least commotion, and why she was death on anyone she caught fooling around with him.

But it wasn't going to work. W.E. wasn't a fluted antique cup in Mrs Nevins's china cupboard. He was a kid – a foster kid. And if he didn't toughen up, what would happen to him when there was no Trotter to look after him?

So Gilly asked him, 'What do you do when somebody socks you?'

His squinty little eyes went wild behind the glasses.

'I'm not going to hit you. I was just wondering what you do.'

He stuck his right index fingers into his mouth and began to tug at the nail.

She took out the finger and studied his stubby-nailed hand for a minute. 'Nothing wrong with this, I can see. Ever think of smacking them back?'

He shook his head wide-eyed.

'You going to go through life letting people pick on you?'

He hung his head. The finger went back in.

'Look, William Ernest' – she bent over close to his ear and whispered hoarsely into it – 'I'm going to teach you how to fight. No charge or anything. Then when some big punk comes up to you and tries to start something, you can just let them have it.'

His finger dropped from his mouth as he stared at her, unbelieving.

'You hear how I fought six boys one day – all by myself?'

He nodded solemnly.

'Before I get through with you, you're going to do the same thing. *Pow! Pow! Pow! Pow! Pow! Pow!*' She landed six imaginary punches sending six imaginary bullies flying.

'*Pow*,' he echoed softly, tentatively doubling up his fist and giving a feeble swing.

'First thing, when somebody yells at you, don't throw your hands up' – she imitated him – 'and act like you think they're going to kill you.'

'*Pow?*' He swung his little fist in a kind of question mark.

'Naw, not *first* thing. See, they may not be even meaning to hit you. First thing is, you take a deep breath –' She filled her diaphragm and waited while he tried to imitate her, his ribs poking through his shirt. 'Then you yell like this: *Get the hell outa my way!*'

Before the sentence was out, Trotter was filling the doorway like the wrath of God Almighty.

'OK, OK,' Gilly said. 'Leave out the hell part. The main thing –'

'What are you kids doing? I thought I was paying you to help William Ernest with his reading?'

'Naw. This is on my own time. No charge.'

Trotter looked anxiously at W.E. He was standing on tiptoe, fists clenched, eyes squeezed shut in his red face, sucking in a huge breath.

'*Get the hell out my way!*' He turned to Gilly, smiling. 'Was that good, Gilly?'

'Better leave the hell part out in front of Trotter. But that was pretty good for a start. Really not bad.'

'Gilly,' said Trotter.

'Look, Trotter. He's got to learn to take care of himself, and I'm the best damn – the best teacher around.'

Trotter just went on standing in the doorway as though she couldn't think what to do next, when the little guy marched over to her, put his fists up in front of her huge bosom, took in a breath, and said squeakily, 'Get out my way.'

Tears started in the woman's eyes. She threw her arms around W.E. and bear-hugged him.

'I was just practising, Trotter. I didn't mean you.'

'I know, William Ernest, honey,' she said. 'I know.'

'He's got to learn to take care of himself in the world, Trotter.'

The big woman wiped her face with her apron and sniffed. 'Don't I know that, baby?' She patted the boy and straightened up. 'How 'bout you finishing this lesson outside? I don't b'lieve it's something I want to listen to.'

'C'mon, Gilly.' William Ernest slid around Trotter and started for the back door. '*Pow! Pow!*' they could hear him exploding softly down the hall.

'I'm not going to teach him to pick on people,' Gilly said, 'just how to take care of himself. He can't come hiding behind your skirt every time someone looks at him cross-eyed.'

'I s'pose not.'

'Even real mothers can't watch out for kids the rest of their lives, and you're just his foster mother.'

'So they keep telling me.'

Gilly hadn't meant to be cruel, but she needed to make Trotter understand. 'If he knows how to read and how to stick up for himself, he'll be OK.'

'You got it all figured out, ain't you, Gilly, honey?' She relaxed into a smile. 'Well, I ain't stopping your boxing lessons. I just don't care to watch.'

Boxing lessons? The woman was a throwback to another century. Gilly started to pass her at the door, but as she brushed by the big body, Trotter grabbed her and planted a wet kiss on her forehead. One hand went up automatically to wipe the spot, but a look at Trotter's face, and Gilly stopped her arm midway.

'Don't know what got into me,' Trotter mumbled, trying to turn it into a joke. 'I know you don't allow no kissing. Sometimes I just haul off and go crazy.'

'At Sunday school Miss Applegate calls it demon possession.'

'Does she now? Demon possession, is it?' She began to laugh so hard, Gilly could feel the boards vibrating under her feet. 'Demon possession – Mercy, girl, I'd have to catch me a jet to keep one step ahead of you. Well – you better get going before the devil grabs me one more time.'

She waved her hand to land a mock spank on Gilly's bottom, but by the time it swept the air, Gilly's bottom along with the rest of her was well down the hall.

# The Visitor

The week before Thanksgiving, Mr Randolph came down with the flu. It wasn't a bad case as flu goes, but he was an old man, and any kind of sickness, as Trotter said, was harder on the old. So with many rest stops for Trotter to recapture her wind, she and Gilly brought the rollaway cot down from the attic and set it up in the dining room, turning the never-used room into a sickroom for Mr Randolph.

There had been a great discussion as to whether big lawyer son should be notified. Mr Randolph was sure that if his son knew he was sick, he would be snatched away to Virginia never to return again. Trotter recognized this appalling possibility, but maintained that there was some moral obligation to inform next of kin when one took to one's bed.

'Suppose he just shows up one day and finds you sick – then he won't trust you no more. He's sure to take you away then.'

But Mr Randolph thought it worth the risk, and they had compromised by having Mr Randolph move in, so Trotter could keep a close eye on him.

'Now what happens if you die on me?'

'I promise not to die in your house. You have my solemn oath.'

'Gilly, if he looks peaky, we carry him next door as fast as we can go. I ain't gonna be sued by no big Virginia lawyer.'

Mr Randolph raised up off the rollaway. 'If I die on you, you can sue me, Mrs Trotter. You can take me for every cent I have.' He lay back, giggling and gasping.

'Humph, every cent. You won't even have no social security if you're dead. Better not die, that's all I got to say.'

'I promise not to die, but with these two beautiful ladies nursing me, I may decide to remain ill for a long, long time.'

'Well, that's a chance I got to take, beautiful as I am. But if you ain't well a week from today, you're gonna miss out on the turkey and stuffings.'

So Mr Randolph swore a solemn oath to be well by Thanksgiving. As it turned out, he was a little better, but by then both Trotter and William Ernest were down with the bug.

Trotter fought going to bed, but her fever was high, and she was too dizzy to stand up. Despite her protests, Gilly stayed home from school Tuesday and Wednesday to nurse the three of them, and Thanksgiving Day found her exhausted from going up and down the stairs and from bedside to bedside.

It occurred to her that if she could get sick, too, no one would blame her for collapsing, but, of course, she didn't catch anything, except irritability from not sleeping properly and worrying. She called Mr Randolph's doctor, Trotter's doctor, and the paediatrician, but no one gave her any help. The patients were to stay in bed and take aspirin for the fever.

Gilly chopped an aspirin in half with the butcher knife for William Ernest. One piece flew out of sight under the stove and the other piece, which she got down the boy's throat with no little difficulty, came up again promptly, along with the bowl of soup she'd coaxed down earlier. She was afraid to try any more aspirin.

Trotter told her to wipe his face and arms and legs with a cold cloth, which seemed to help the fever a little, but the child was still miserable, and clean as she might, the smell of old vomit hung in the room.

The whole house was a mess, in fact. Even rooms like the living room and kitchen, which nobody but she went into, began to look as though they had been bombed. She was simply too whipped to pick up after herself.

By Thursday she couldn't have cared less about Thanksgiving. The turkey Trotter had bought was relentlessly defrosting on the refrigerator shelf, but there was nothing else to remind her as she sat at the kitchen table dressed in jeans and a shrunken T-shirt, chewing her late breakfast of bologna sandwich, that the rest of the nation would soon be feasting and celebrating.

The doorbell rang. She jumped at the sound. Her first fear was that lawyer son had not believed Mr Randolph's excuses for not coming to Virginia for Thanksgiving and had come to get him. Then, with annoyance, she realized that it was probably Agnes Stokes, sneaking around to find out why Gilly had skipped school for two days.

But when she opened the door, it was to a small, plump woman whose grey hair peaked out from under a close-fitting black felt hat. She wore black gloves and a black-and-tweed overcoat, which was a little too long to be fashionable, and carried a slightly worn black alligator bag over one arm. The woman, who was an inch or so shorter than she was, looked up into Gilly's face with a sort of peculiar expression, whether frightened or hungry, Gilly couldn't have said. At any rate, it made her shift uncomfortably and push at her bangs until she remembered two of Trotter's trusty sentences for emergency use and offered both of them.

'We're not buying anything today, thank you, and we're faithful members of the Baptist Church.' She hurried to close the door.

'No, wait please,' the lady said. 'Galadriel – Hopkins?'

Gilly yanked the door back open. 'Who are you?' she blurted out, as awkwardly as William Ernest might have.

'I'm' – it was the woman's turn to look uncomfortable. 'I'm – I suppose I'm your grandmother.'

Somehow Gilly would have been less surprised if the woman had said fairy godmother.

'May I come in?'

Dumbly Gilly stepped back and let her.

The sound of snoring poured forth from the dining room. Gilly willed the woman not to look, not to stare at the funny little brown face poked up above the faded quilt, the mouth gaped and trembling with each noisy breath. But, of course, the woman looked, jerked her head slightly at the sight, and then turned quickly back to Gilly.

'Gilly, honey, who is it?' Damn! Trotter must have heard the bell.

'OK, Trotter, I got it,' Gilly yelled, as she tugged at her shrunken T-shirt (the last half-clean one) and tried to make it cover her navel. 'Want to sit down?' she asked the visitor.

'Yes. Please.'

Gilly led the way into the living room and backed up to the couch, sticking a hand out toward the brown chair.

*Plunk*. They both sat down in unison like string puppets, the lady right on the edge of the chair so that her short feet could touch the floor.

'So –' The woman was bobbing her little black hat. Did anyone in the world wear hats these days? 'So –'

Gilly was trying to take it in. This – this little old lady in the old-fashioned hat and coat – was Courtney's mother? In all Gilly's fantasies, Courtney had never had a mother. She had always been – existing from before time – like a goddess in perpetual perfection.

'I'm right, aren't I? You are Galadriel?' Her voice was Southern but smooth, like silk to Trotter's burlap.

Gilly nodded.

'My daughter –' The woman fumbled in her purse and brought out a letter. 'My daughter left home many –' She snapped the purse shut and raised her eyes to meet Gilly's puzzled ones. '– many years ago. I – my husband and I never ... I'm sorry ...'

Helplessly Gilly watched the little woman stumbling for words, trying to tell a painful story and not knowing how.

'My husband –' She tried to smile. 'Your grandfather died – nearly twelve years ago.'

Perhaps she should say something, thought Gilly. 'Jeez, that's too bad.'

'Yes. Yes, it was.' The woman was pushing hard against the words to keep from crying. Gilly knew the trick. Oh, boy, how well she knew that one. 'We – I tried to contact Courtney, your mother, at the time, of course. But – I was not able to. In fact –' The pitch of her voice went up. She stopped trying to talk and took a handkerchief from her purse, barely touching each nostril before putting it away.

Go ahead and blow, honey. It'll make you feel better. Trotter would have said it, but Gilly couldn't quite get it out.

'As a matter of fact –' The woman had recovered herself enough to continue. 'As a matter of fact, this letter – this letter is the first direct word we've – I've had from my daughter in thirteen years.'

'You're kidding,' said Gilly. She felt sorry even though the woman's pain didn't seem to have anything to do with her.

'I didn't even know she'd had a ba – Wouldn't you think she'd want her own mother to know she'd had a baby?'

This was obviously the point where she, Gilly, was

supposed to come into the story, but it still seemed far too remote, like something that had happened once to a friend of a friend. She tried to nod in a sympathetic manner.

'Gilly. I called you and called you.' William Ernest stood clutching the doorway for support, his face still flushed with fever. He was dressed in his long greyish-white underwear. At the sight of a stranger, he stopped dead.

The woman looked at him once hard; then as she had done with Mr Randolph, she looked quickly away.

'I'm sorry, W.E.,' Gilly said. 'I didn't hear you call me. What's the matter?' As soon as she asked, she knew. His long johns were wet all down the front. Gilly jumped up. 'Scuse me, I'll be right back.' She hustled the boy back to his room, as fast as you could hustle a boy who was still weak from fever and lack of food. It was hard to be patient with him on the stairs. 'You shouldn't have come down-stairs, William Ernest. You're sick.'

'I wet,' he said sadly. 'I couldn't help it.'

She sighed. 'I know. When you're sick, you just can't help it.' She got him the last clean underwear, which was short and wouldn't be as warm, and changed his sheets. She took a dry blanket off her own bed. He climbed in and turned his back to her at once, his strength exhausted.

'Gilly, honey,' Trotter called drowsily as Gilly passed her door. 'You got company down there?'

'Just playing the TV.' Gilly smoothed her hair and tug-ged again at her shirt as she went down the stairs. She knew she looked a wreck. She must have shocked the poor old lady right out of her socks.

The woman gave a weak smile and nodded when Gilly came in. 'You poor little thing,' she said.

Gilly looked behind to see if W.E. had followed her down.

'Bless your heart.' There was no one else around.

'Me?'

'Courtney didn't exaggerate. I'm just so glad you wrote her, my dear. How could they have put you in such a place?'

'Me?' What was the woman talking about? What place?

'I know I shouldn't have burst in upon you like this, but I felt I had to see for myself before I talked with your caseworker. Will you forgive me, my dear, for –'

There was a heavy thump, thump, thumping on the stairs. Both of them sat stark still and listened as it drew inexorably nearer.

'*Ohhh!*' The little lady gasped.

Swaying in the doorway was a huge barefoot apparition in striped men's pyjamas, grey hair cascading over its shoulders, a wild look in its eyes.

'I forgot!' It was moaning as it swayed. 'I forgot!' It grabbed frantically at the woodwork. 'I forgot.'

Gilly sprang to her feet. 'What did you forget, dammit?'

'The turkey' – Trotter was almost sobbing now – 'Fifteen dollars and thirty-eight cents, and I let it go to rot.' She gave no sign that she noticed the visitor.

'Nothing's gone to rot. I would have smelled it, wouldn't I?' – Gilly couldn't help sneaking a sideways glance at the little woman, who looked almost as frightened as W.E. did when he spied a new word in his reading book – 'Go back to bed, Trotter. I'll put it right in the oven.'

The huge woman made an effort to obey, but nearly fell down just trying to turn around. 'I better sit a minute,' she panted. 'My head's light.'

Gilly grabbed the back of the striped pyjamas with both hands and half dragged, half supported the faltering frame toward the couch. But she knew – just as one knows when piling on one final block that the tower will fall – she knew they couldn't make it.

'Oh, mercy!' Trotter gave a little cry as she came crashing down, pinning Gilly to the rug beneath her. The woman lay there, flapping on her back like a giant over-turned tortoise. 'Well, I done it now.' She gave a short hysterical giggle. 'Squished you juicy.'

'What? What is it?' The third night-clothed actor had made his entrance.

'You awright, ain't you, Gilly, honey?' asked Trotter, and without waiting for an answer, 'S'awright, Mr Randolph.'

'But someone fell. I heard someone fall.'

'Yeah, I fell awright.' Trotter was rocking her huge trunk in a vain effort to get to her feet. 'But it's OK, ain't it, Gilly, honey?'

'Just roll, Trotter,' said a muffled voice. 'Roll over and you'll be off me.'

'What's that? What's that?' Mr Randolph squeaked.

'It's poor little Gilly.' Trotter grunted and with a su-preme *ahhhhhhh* rolled off onto the floor.

'Miss Gilly?' he was asking anxiously.

'I'm OK, Mr Randolph.' Gilly got up, dusted herself off, then took him by the hand. 'Let's get you back into bed.'

By the time she returned from the dining room, Trotter had somehow hoisted herself into a sitting position on the couch, and dizzily clutching the cushions with both hands, had found herself face to face with a white-faced stranger.

'You said wasn't no one here,' she accused Gilly.

The visitor, for her part, was teetering on the absolute brink of the brown chair in what Gilly took to be a state of total shock. But the small lady proved capable of speech. 'I think I'd better go,' she said, standing up. 'I don't seem to have come at a very good time.'

Gilly followed her to the door, eager to get her out of the looney bin the house had suddenly become.

'I'm glad to have met you,' she said as politely as she could. She had no wish for the woman to think poorly of her. After all, she was – or, at least, she claimed to be – Courtney's mother.

The woman paused, resisting Gilly's efforts to hurry her out the door. She reached over abruptly and pecked Gilly on the cheek. 'I'll get you out of here soon,' she whispered fiercely. 'I promise you, I will.'

Fatigue had made Gilly stupid. She simply nodded and closed the door quickly behind the little form. It wasn't until she'd gotten Trotter back in bed and was putting the turkey in the oven that the woman's meaning came clear.

Oh, my god.

Well, it didn't matter what the woman thought. Miss Ellis could explain about today. No one could make her leave here, not when everyone needed her so. Besides – Trotter wouldn't let them take her. 'Never,' she had said. 'Never, never, never.'

# Never
# and Other Cancelled Promises

Dread lay on Gilly's stomach like a dead fish on the beach. Even when you don't look at it, the stink pervades everything. She finally made herself admit the fact that it was her own letter that had driven Courtney to get in touch with her mother after a silence of thirteen years. What had it said? She couldn't even remember what the letter had said. And Courtney's letter had, in turn, brought the little lady up from Virginia to spy her out.

And now what? It was not at all the way she'd imagined the ending. In Gilly's story Courtney herself came sweeping in like a goddess queen, reclaiming the long-lost princess. There was no place in this dream for dumpy old-fashioned ladies with Southern speech, or barefoot fat women in striped pyjamas, or blind old black men who recited poetry by heart and snored with their mouths open – or crazy, heart-ripping little guys who went '*pow*' and still wet their stupid beds.

But she had done it. Like Bluebeard's wife, she'd opened the forbidden door and someday she would have to look inside.

By Saturday night, when the turkey was finally upon the kitchen table with the four of them gathered gratefully around it, there was still no word from either Miss Ellis or the Commonwealth of Virginia.

Trotter and W.E. looked deathly white, and Mr Randolph was the shade of ashes, but they had thrown off the crankiness of their illness and were eating the cold dry meat with chirpy expressions of delight.

'I declare, Miss Gilly, you are the only person I know who can rival Mrs Trotter's culinary skill.' A statement Gilly knew for a bald-faced if kindly intended lie.

'The potatoes are lumpy,' she responded, doing some tardy mashing with the tines of her fork.

'Mine ain't lumpy,' W.E. whispered loyally.

'They're just fine, Gilly, honey. I think you gave yourself the only lump in the pot. Mine's smooth as ice cream. I don't know how long it's been' – Trotter paused, head tilted as though reaching far back into her memory – 'I don't think food's tasted this good to me since . . . since before Melvin took sick the last time.' She beamed, having delivered the ultimate compliment.

Gilly blushed despite herself. They were all liars, but how could you mind?

'Gilly, honey' – Trotter stopped a forkful in midair – 'who was that woman come here the other day? What she want?'

Now it was Gilly's turn to lie. 'Well, I think she was about to ask us to join her church, but before I could tell her about being faithful Baptists, all of you come roaring in looking like three-day-old death. Scared her straight out the door.'

'Me, too?' asked W.E.

'You were the worst one, William Ernest. She saw you standing there, all tall and white and skinny, calling my name, "*Gi—— lyeeeeeee. Gi —— lyeeeeeee.*" She nearly swallowed her dentures.'

'Really?'

'Would I lie?'

'*Pow*,' he said.

'Well, she sure got up and hightailed it when I come in and bulldozed poor Gilly clean through the carpet.' Trotter snickered. 'I reckon she thought she was fixing to be next.'

'What you do?' asked W.E.

'I fell smack down on Gilly and couldn't get back up for the life of me.'

Mr Randolph was giggling. 'I was awakened by a terrible crash. I came as fast as I could . . .'

'Then all you could hear was this little squeak, "Roll off me, Trotter. Roll off me!"' Trotter repeated herself getting nearer to hysterics with each repetition.'"Roll off me!"'

'Did you roll off her?'

'Mercy, boy, it weren't that easy. I huffed and I puffed . . .'

'And you blew the house down!' William Ernest pounded the table, and they all laughed until the tears came, taking turns to cry out, 'Roll off me!' and 'Not by the hair of my chinny-chin-chin!'

'Roll off me!' was not what Gilly remembered saying, but it didn't matter. It was so good to have them all well, laughing, and eating together. Besides, in their merriment, the little grey-haired lady had slipped from their thoughts.

But Monday came, and the long holiday weekend was over. Gilly, armed with an absence excuse that looked more like a commendation for bravery in battle, and William Ernest, cheerful but pale, went back to school. Mr Randolph moved home again, and Trotter, taking time to rest every few minutes, began to straighten up the house. And, as Gilly learned later, by the time Miss Ellis reached her desk at twelve after nine, there was already a note upon it directing her to call a Mrs Rutherford Hopkins in Loudoun County, Virginia.

Gilly had waited after school at William Ernest's classroom door. She didn't want him taking on any fights while he was still wobbly from the flu, and she knew, with her reputation, that no one would sneeze in his direction if he were walking with her.

Agnes Stokes danced along beside them, trying to entice Gilly to join her in a trip to the deli, but Gilly was too intent on getting W.E. home.

'Or we could go to my house and call people on the phone and breathe weird.'

'Come off it, Agnes. That is so dumb.'

'No, it really scares 'em. I've had 'em screaming all over the place at me.'

'It is dumb, Agnes. Dumb, dumb, dumb.'

'You always say that when you don't think it up yourself.'

'Right. I don't think up dumb things.'

'C'mon, Gilly. Let's do *something*. You ain't done nothing with me for a long time.'

'My family's been sick.'

Agnes sneered. 'What family? Everybody knows...'

'My brother.' At this William Ernest raised his head up proudly. 'My mother. And my – uncle.'

'Gilly Hopkins. *That* is the dumbest idea...'

Gilly spun around and jammed her nose down onto Agnes's face, her mouth going sideways and narrow exactly like Humphrey Bogart's on TV. 'You want to discuss this further – sweetheart?'

Agnes backed up. 'It's too dumb to talk about even,' she said, still backing. 'Really dumb.'

William Ernest slid close to Gilly so they couldn't help touching as they walked. 'Bet I could beat her up,' he whispered.

'Yeah,' Gilly said. 'But don't bother. Hell, it wouldn't be fair. You against that poor little puny thing.'

Trotter was at the door, opening it before they reached the porch. Gilly went cold. You could tell something was badly wrong by the way the woman's smile twisted and her body sagged.

Sure enough. Miss Ellis was sitting on the brown chair. This time the two women had not been fighting, just waiting for her. Gilly's heart gave a little spurt and flopped over like a dud rocket. She sat down quickly on the couch and hugged herself to keep from shaking.

Suddenly Miss Ellis began to speak, her voice bright and fake like a laxative commercial: 'Well, I've got some rather astounding news for you, Gilly.' Gilly hugged herself tighter. The announcement of 'news' had never meant anything in her life except a new move. 'Your mother...'

'My mother's coming?' She was sorry immediately for the outburst. Miss Ellis's eyebrows launched into the twitchy dance they always seemed to at the mention of the words, 'my mother'.

'No.' Twitch, twitch. 'Your mother is still in California. But your grandmother...'

What have I to do with her?

'...your mother's mother called the office this morning, and then drove up all the way from Virginia to see me.'

Gilly stole a look at Trotter, who was sitting bolt upright at the far end of the couch, rubbing W.E.'s back, her hand up under his jacket and her eyes like those of a bear on a totem pole.

'She and your mother' – twitch – 'want you to go with her.'

'With who?'

'With your grandmother. *Permanently*.' The social worker seemed to be dangling that last word before Gilly's nose, as if expecting her to jump up on her hind legs and dance for it.

Gilly leaned back. What did they take her for? 'I don't want to live with her,' she said.

'Gilly, you've been saying ever since you were old enough to talk...'

'I never said I wanted to live with *her!* I said I wanted to live with my *mother.* She's not my mother. I don't even know her!'

'You don't know your mother, either.'

'I do, too! I remember her! Don't tell me what I remember and what I don't!'

Miss Ellis suddenly looked tired. 'God help the children of the flower children,' she said.

'I remember her.'

'Yes.' The pretty face grew sharp with tension, as the social worker leaned forward. 'Your mother wants you to go to your grandmother's. I talked to her long distance.'

'Didn't she tell you she wanted me to come to California like she wrote me?'

'No, she said she wanted you to go to your grandmother's house.'

'They can't make me go there.'

Gently, 'Yes, Gilly, they can.'

She felt as though the walls were squeezing in on her; she looked around wildly for some way to escape. She fixed on Trotter.

'Trotter won't let them take me, will you, Trotter?'

Trotter flinched but kept on looking wooden-faced at Miss Ellis and rubbing W.E.'s back.

'Trotter! Look at me! You said you'd never let me go. I heard you.' She was yelling at the totem pole now. 'Never! Never! Never! That's what you said!' She was on her feet stamping and screaming. The two women watched her, but numbly as though she were behind glass and there was no way that they could reach in to her.

It was William Ernest who broke through. He slid from under Trotter's big hand and ran to Gilly, snatched the band of her jacket, and pulled on it until she stopped screaming and stood still. She looked down into his little near-sighted eyes, full of tears behind the thick lenses.

'Don't cry, Gilly.'

'I'm not crying' – she jerked her jacket out of his hands – 'I'm yelling!' He froze, his hands up as though the jacket were still between his fingers.

'Oh, hell, kid.' She grabbed his two fists. 'It's gonna be OK.' She sighed and sat down. He sat down next to her, so close that she could feel the warmth of him from her arm through her thigh. It gave her the strength to look up again defiantly.

Miss Ellis was looking at the two of them like a bird watcher onto a rare species. But the big woman – Gilly could see the pain breaking up the totem-pole stare – Trotter shuddered to her feet like an old circus elephant.

'You tell the child what's got to be done. C'mon, William Ernest, honey.' She stuck out her big hand. 'We ain't helping here.' When he hesitated, she reached down and gently pulled him to his feet. They closed the door behind them, leaving Gilly cold and alone.

'You seem to have changed your mind about a lot of things.'

'So?'

'So you goofed it, right?' – Gilly didn't answer. What did it matter? – 'I'd really like to know what you wrote that fool letter for.'

'You wouldn't understand.'

'You bet I wouldn't. I don't understand why a smart girl like you goes around booby-trapping herself. You could have stayed here indefinitely, you know. They're both crazy about you.' Miss Ellis shook her long blond hair back off her shoulders. 'Well, it's done now. Your grandmother will come to pick you up at my office tomorrow. I'll come about nine to get you.'

'Tomorrow?'

'Gilly, believe me, it's better. Waiting around is no good in these situations.'

'But I got school' – not even a good-bye for cool, beautiful Miss Harris or silly little Agnes?

'They'll send your records on.' Miss Ellis stood up and began to button her coat. 'I must admit that last month when you ran away, I thought, Uh-oh, here we go again, but I was wrong, Gilly. You've done well here. I'm very pleased.'

'Then let me stay.' Galadriel Hopkins had rarely come so close to begging.

'I can't,' Miss Ellis said simply. 'It's out of my hands.'

# The Going

For dinner that night Trotter fried chicken so crisp it would crackle when you bit it, and she beat the potatoes into creamy peaks with the electric mixer. She had made Mr Randolph his favourite green beans with ham bits and for Gilly and W.E. there was a fruit salad with baby marshmallows. The sweet-sour smell of cherry pie filled the kitchen where the four of them sat around the table without appetite for food or speech.

Only William Ernest cried, big, silent tears catching in the corners of the frame of his glasses and then spilling down his cheeks. Mr Randolph, smaller and thinner than ever, sat forward on his chair, with a shy, half smile on his face, which meant he was just about to say something but he never quite got it out. Trotter was breathing as hard as if she had just climbed the stairs. She kept rearranging the serving dishes as though just about to offer seconds, but since the four plates were still piled high, the gesture was useless.

Gilly watched her and tried to decide how much Miss Ellis had told her. Did she know the Thanksgiving visitor was Gilly's grandmother? Did Trotter know – she hoped not – about the crazy letter? She still couldn't remember what she had said in the letter. Had she said W.E. was retarded? Her mind blanked in self-defence. Oh, god, don't let Trotter know. I never meant to hurt them. I just wanted – what had she wanted? A home – but Trotter had tried to give her that. Permanence – Trotter had wanted to give her that as well. No, what she wanted was something Trotter had no power over. To stop being a 'foster child', the quotation marks dragging the phrase down, almost drowning it. To be real without any quotation marks. To belong and to possess. To be herself, to be the swan, to be the ugly duckling no longer – Cap O'Rushes, her disguise thrown off – Cinderella with both slippers on her feet – Snow White beyond the dwarfs – Galadriel Hopkins, come into her own.

But there was to be no coming, only a going.

'If you all don't start eating this supper, I'm gonna' – Trotter stopped, fishing around for a proper threat. She took a deep breath – 'Jump up and down on the table, squawking like a two-hundred-pound lovesick chicken!'

'Really?' William Ernest took off his glasses and wiped them on his pants to prepare for a better view.

Mr Randolph's fixed smile crumbled into a nervous titter. Gilly swallowed to clear her clogged-up throat and took a large noisy bite of her drumstick.

'Now, that's more like it.' Trotter patted her shiny face with the tail of her apron. 'This was supposed to be a party, not some kinda funeral.' She turned to Mr Randolph and half shouted. 'Gilly's folks are from Loudoun County, Mr Randolph.'

'Oh, that's lovely, lovely country, Miss Gilly. Real Virginia horse country.'

'You got horses, Gilly?'

'I don't know, W.E.' She found it hard to imagine the little pudgy lady on horseback, but who could tell?

'Can I see 'em?'

'Sure. If I got 'em, you can see 'em.'

She caught a flicked warning from Trotter over the boy's head, but Gilly ignored it. 'It's not as if I'm going to Hong Kong. Hell. You can just hop on a bus and come to see me – any time.'

Trotter was shaking her head. She put her hand over on W.E.'s shoulder. 'When folks leave, William Ernest, hon-ey, they gotta have a chance to settle in and get used to things. Sometimes it's best not to go visiting, right away.'

If you mean 'never', Trotter, say so. Is that it? Will I never see the three of you again? Are you going to stand by and let them rip me out and fold me up and fly me away? Leave me a string, Trotter, a thread, at least. Dammit. She'd tie her own.

'I'll write you, W.E. The mailman will bring you a letter with your name on it. Just for you.'

'Me?' he said.

'Nobody else.' She looked belligerently at Trotter, but Trotter was so busy making the meat platter and the salad bowl switch places that the expression was wasted.

After supper Gilly did her homework, knowing it was useless, that Miss Harris would never see the neat figures, row on row, that proved that Gilly Hopkins had met and mastered the metric system. When she finished, she thought briefly of calling Agnes, but what should she say? 'Good-bye' when she'd never really said 'hello'? Poor Agnes, what would become of her? Would she stomp herself angrily through the floor, or would someone's kiss turn her magically into a princess? Alas, Agnes, the world is woefully short on frog smoochers.

No, she wouldn't call, but maybe, someday, she'd write. William Ernest walked Mr Randolph home and returned carrying *The Oxford Book of English Verse* for Gilly – a farewell present from Mr Randolph.

'Gilly, honey, do you know what kind of present that is?'

Gilly could guess.

'Like he tore a piece off hisself and gave it to you.'

Gilly ran a finger over the wrinkled brown leather, which could almost have been a piece of Mr Randolph, but the observation seemed too raw, so she kept it to herself.

She waited for Trotter to puff up the stairs to take W.E. to bed before she began to look for the poem:

> Our birth is but a sleep and a forgetting:
> The Soul that rises with us, our life's Star,
>   Hath had elsewhere its setting
>     And cometh from afar:
>   Not in entire forgetfulness,
>   And not in utter nakedness,
> But trailing clouds of glory do we come
>   From God, who is our home.

She didn't understand it any more than she had the first time. If birth was a sleep and a forgetting, what was death? But she didn't really care. It was the sounds she loved – the sounds that turned and fell in kaleidoscopic wonder.

'And not in utter nakedness.' Who would have thought those five words could fall into such a pattern of light? And her favourite 'But trailing clouds of glory do we come'. Was it all the *l*'s that did it or the mental picture that streaked cometlike across the unfocused lens of her mind?

'From God, who is our home.' Again the lens was unfocused. Was that God with the huge lap smelling of baby powder? Or was that home?

She awoke in the night, trying to remember the dream that had awakened her. It was a sad one, or why did her heart feel like a lump of poorly mashed potatoes? It was something about Courtney. Courtney coming to get her, and then, having seen her, turning away sorrowing: 'Never, never, never.' But the voice was Trotter's.

She began to cry softly into her pillow, not knowing why or for whom. Maybe for all the craziness she had tried so hard to manage and was never quite able to.

And then Trotter was beside her, making the bedsprings

screech at the burden of her body. She leaned over, her hair, loose from its daytime knot, falling across Gilly's own hair.

'You OK, baby?'

Gilly turned to face her, this mountain smelling of Johnson's baby powder and perspiration. In the dark, she could hardly make out the lines on Trotter's face.

'Yeah,' she sniffed. 'OK.'

Trotter took the hem of the striped pyjama top and gently wiped Gilly's eyes and nose. 'I ain't supposed to let on how I feel. I ain't got no blood claim on you, and the Lord in Heaven knows I want you to have a good life with your own people. But' – her huge bass voice broke up into little squeaky pieces – 'but it's killing me to see you go.' The whole mammoth body began to shake with giant sobs.

Gilly sat up and put her arms as far as they could go around Trotter. 'I'm not going to go,' she cried. 'They can't make me!'

Trotter quieted at once. 'No, baby. You got to go. Lord forgive me for making it harder for you.'

'I'll come back and see you all the time.'

Trotter stuck her big warm hand underneath Gilly's pyjama top and began to rub her back, the way Gilly had often seen her rub W.E.'s. 'No, Gilly, baby. It don't work that way. Like I tried to tell you at supper. Once the tugboat takes you out to the ocean liner, you got to get all the way on board. Can't straddle both decks.'

'I could,' said Gilly.

The big hand paused in its healing journey around and up and down her back, then began again as Trotter said softly, 'Don't make it harder for us, baby.'

Perhaps Gilly should have protested further, but instead she gave herself over to the rhythmic stroking under whose comfort she wished she could curl up her whole body like a tiny sightless kitten and forget about the rest of the whole stinking world.

She could almost forget, lying there in the silence, letting the soothing warmth of the big hand erase all the aching. At last, overcome with drowsiness, she slid down into the bed.

Trotter pulled the covers up around Gilly's chin and patted them and her.

'You make me proud, hear?'

'OK,' she murmured and was asleep.

# Jackson, Virginia

The ride in Mrs Hopkins's ten-year-old Buick station wagon to Jackson, Virginia, took just over an hour. To Gilly it seemed like a hundred years. Every other time she'd moved, she'd been able to think of the destination as a brief stop along the way, but this one was the end of the road. Always before she had known she could stand anything, because someday soon Courtney would come and take her home. But now she had to face the fact that Courtney had not come. She had sent someone else in her place. Perhaps Courtney would never come. Perhaps Courtney did not want to come.

The heaviness dragged her down. What was she doing here in this old car with this strange woman who surely didn't want her, who had only taken her out of some stupid idea of duty, when she could be home with Trotter and William Ernest and Mr Randolph who really wanted her? Who – could she dare the word, even to herself? – who loved her.

And she loved them. Oh, hell. She'd spent all her life – at least all of it since the Dixons went to Florida and left her behind – making sure she didn't care about anyone but Courtney. She had known that it never pays to attach yourself to something that is likely to blow away. But in Thompson Park, she'd lost her head. She loved those stupid people.

'Would you like to turn on the radio?'

'No, that's all right.'

'I'm not familiar with the latest music, but I don't really mind, as long as it's not too loud.'

Can't you just leave me alone?

There were several miles of silence before the woman tried again: 'Miss Ellis seems like a nice person.'

Gilly shrugged. 'She's OK, I guess.'

'She – uh – seems to think I got a rather wrong impression of that foster home she'd put you in.'

Something dark and hot began to bubble up inside of Gilly. 'They were all sick last week,' she said.

'I see.'

How in the hell could you see?

'Miss Ellis tried to tell me that you had really liked it there – despite everything. From your letter –'

That damn letter. 'I lie a lot,' Gilly said tightly.

'Oh.' A quick side glance and then back to the windshield. The woman was so short she was almost peering through the top of the steering wheel. Gilly saw her small hands tighten on the wheel as she said, 'I'd hoped you'd be glad to come with me. I'm sorry.'

If you're sorry, turn this old crate around and take me back. But, of course, the woman didn't.

The house was on the edge of the village. It was a little larger, a little older, and considerably cleaner than Trotter's. No horses for W.E. Oh, well, she hadn't really expected any.

'I thought you might like to have Courtney's room. What do you think?'

'Anything is all right.' But when she got to the door of Courtney's room, she hung back. Everything was pink with a four-poster canopied bed complete with stuffed animals and dolls. She couldn't make herself go in.

'It's all right, my dear. It's a big house. You may choose.'

The room which she found most to her liking had a bunk bed with brown corduroy spreads and models of airplanes hanging on delicate wires from the ceiling. In a metal-wire wastebasket was a basketball and a football and a baseball mitt still cradling a stained and scruffed-up ball. The grandmother explained quietly without her having to ask that it was the room of Chadwell, Courtney's older brother, a pilot who had one day crashed into the steaming jungles of Vietnam. Nonetheless, his room seemed less haunted than his sister's.

'Would you like me to help you unpack?'

Inside her head, she was screaming, 'I don't need any help!' but for Trotter's sake, she said only, 'No, I can do it.'

They ate lunch in the dining room with real monogrammed silver off silver-rimmed china set on lace mats.

The woman caught Gilly eyeing the layout. 'I hope you don't mind my celebrating a little.' She seemed to be apologizing. 'I usually eat in the kitchen since I've been alone.'

The word 'alone' twanged in Gilly's head. She knew what it meant to be alone. But only since Thompson Park did she understand a little what it meant to have people and then lose them. She looked at the person who was smiling shyly at her, who had lost husband, son, daughter. That was alone.

As lunch progressed, the woman began almost to chatter, as though she were overcoming her shyness, or forcing herself to. 'I feel very silly saying to you, Tell me all about yourself, but I wish you would. I want to get to know you.'

That's not how you get to know people. Don't you know? You can't talk it out, you got to live into their lives, bad and good. You'll know me soon enough. What I want you to know.

'Miss Ellis says you're very bright.'

'I guess so.'

'Do you want to see about school right away? Or would you rather settle in here first?'

'I don't know. It doesn't matter.'

'I'm afraid you'll get bored just sitting around with me all day. I want you to make friends your own age. I'm sure there are some nice girls your age somewhere around.'

I have never in my life been friends with a 'nice girl'.

'What kinds of things do you enjoy doing?'

Please shut up. I can't stand your trying so hard. 'I don't know. Anything.'

'If you like to read, I still have Chadwell and Courtney's books. There may even be a bicycle in the shed. Do you suppose it's any good after all these years? Would you like a bicycle? I'm sure we could find the money for a bicycle if you'd like one.'

Stop hovering over me. I'll smother.

They did the dishes. Gilly wiped silently while her grandmother nervously put-putted on and on. It didn't seem necessary to answer her questions. She went right on whether or not Gilly bothered to reply. What had happened to the quiet little lady in the car? It was as though someone had turned on a long-unused faucet. The problem was how in the world to get it shut off again. Gilly had to try. She yawned elaborately and stretched.

'Are you tired, dear?'

Gilly nodded. 'I guess I haven't caught up on my sleep. I had to be up a lot last week with everyone sick and all.'

'Oh, my dear. How thoughtless of me! Here I go on and on . . .'

'No. It's all right. I think I'll just go up and lie down, though, if you don't mind.'

'What a good idea. I often lie down a little in the afternoon myself.'

In the quiet of Chadwell's room, Gilly lay back and gazed out the window at the blue expanse of sky. If she lifted up on her elbow she could see the rolling fields beyond the margin of the tiny town, and beyond the hills, the mountains dark and strong. She felt herself loosening. Had Chadwell been homesick for this sight as he dropped his bombs into the jungle? Why would anyone leave such peace for war? Maybe he had to go. Maybe they didn't give him any choice. But Courtney had had a choice. Why had she left? You don't just leave your mother because she talks too much. Why should she leave and not look back a single time – until now?

She must care about me, at least a little. She wrote her mother to come and get me because she was worried about me. Doesn't that prove she cares? Gilly got up and took Courtney's picture out from underneath her T-shirts. How silly. She was in Courtney's house now. Courtney didn't have to hide in a drawer any longer. She propped the picture up against the bureau lamp. Maybe her grandmother would let her buy a frame for it. She sat down on the bed and looked back at Courtney on the bureau. Beautiful, smiling Courtney of the perfect teeth and lovely hair.

But something was wrong. The face didn't fit in this room any more than it had fit in all the others. Oh, Courtney, why did you go away and leave her? Why did you go away and leave me? She jumped up and slid the picture face-down under the T-shirts again.

# She'll Be Riding Six White Horses (When She Comes)

P.O. Box 33
Jackson, Va.
December 5

Dear William Ernest,

Ha! I bet you thought I'd forget. But don't worry. I wouldn't forget you. I have just been so busy looking after the horses I have hardly had a minute to myself. I practically fall into bed I'm so worn out from all the work. Have you ever shovelled horse manure?

Just kidding. Actually, it is a lot of fun. We are getting six of the horses ready to race at the Charles Town track soon, so I have to help them train. I am sure one of them, named Clouds of Glory, is going to win. The prize is about a half a million dollars, so we will be even richer when he does. Not that we need the money, being millionaires and all.

How is school? I bet you zonked Miss McNair with all those new words you learned last month. You should keep in practice by reading out loud to Mr Randolph.

Tell Trotter we have three maids and a cook, but the cook isn't half as good as she is, even though she uses lots of fancy ingredients. (Ha! Bet you knock Miss McNair over when you read her that word.)

Write soon.

Gilly

P.S. My grandmother told me to call her 'Nonnie'. Aren't rich people weird?

Thompson Park Elementary School
Thompson Park, Maryland
December 7

Dear Gilly,

If anyone had told me how much I would miss having you in my class, I'd never have believed it. I hope, however, that you are enjoying your new school and that the people there are enjoying you as well. You might like to know that when I send your records to Virginia, I do not plan to include any samples of your poetry.

You will be receiving soon some paperbacks that I'd been meaning to lend you, but now that you've left us, I want you to keep them as a souvenir of our days together in Harris 6.

I certainly won't forget you even if you never write, but it would be good to hear how you're getting along.

Best wishes,
Barbara Harris


December 10

Dear Gilly,

How are you? I am fine. I liked your letter. I liked your horses. Write me soon.

Love,
William Ernest Teague

P.S. Did you win the race?


P.O. Box 33
Jackson, Virginia
December 15

Dear Miss Harris,

The books by J.R.R. Tolkien came the day after your letter. Now I know who Galadriel was. Do you think Frodo should keep trying to take back the magic ring? I think it would be better if he kept it and took charge of things himself. Do you know what I mean? Anyhow, thank you for the books. They are really exciting.

They help a lot because this school is terrible. Nobody knows anything, including the teachers. I wish I was back in Harris 6.

Your former student,
Gilly Hopkins

P.S. It's OK if you want to call me Galadriel.

December 16

Dear William Ernest,

Of course we won the race. Now we are training for the Kentucky Derby. I guess I will have to miss a lot of school to go to that, but it won't matter. They have already told me that I will probably skip to the ninth grade, because I am so far ahead of all the sixth graders in this dumb school. When you are old enough, I will take you to a horse race. How about that?

Tell Trotter and Mr Randolph hello for me. Are you reading to Mr Randolph like I told you to?

Take care.

Gilly

P.S. Why don't you ask Santa to bring you some karate lessons?

December 17

Dear William Ernest, Trotter, and Mr Randolph,

I just wrote William Ernest yesterday, but now I got some real news. I just heard that my mother is coming on December 23. I know I lie a lot, so you won't believe this, but it is really the truth this time. She is really coming. I hope you all have a Merry Christmas and a Happy New Year.

Galadriel (Gilly) Hopkins

Her mother was really coming. At least Nonnie, who had talked to her on the telephone while Gilly was at school, believed she was. She was due at Dulles Airport at 11 A.M. on December twenty-third. A whole week to wait. Gilly thought she might die waiting. She dulled the agony somewhat by plunging into housecleaning for Nonnie.

Nonnie was all right. She could still chatter Gilly straight into a pounding headache, but she meant well. And then, whenever Gilly would lose patience with her, she'd remember the first day Nonnie had taken her into Jackson Elementary School.

They had marched into the principal's office, and Nonnie had said: 'Margaret, this is my granddaughter, Galadriel Hopkins.'

The principal had raised her eyebrows. She had obviously known Nonnie for years, and this was the first mention she'd ever had of a granddaughter. 'Your granddaughter?' she said giving Gilly's new blouse and jumper the once over. 'Hopkins, did you say?'

You had to hand it to old Nonnie. She didn't blink an eye. 'Yes, I said Hopkins. She's Courtney's child.'

'I see,' said the principal, and you could practically see the wheels spinning in that prissy head of hers. 'I see. Hopkins. Now how do you spell her Christian name?' Had she exaggerated Christian ever so slightly? If so, Nonnie took no notice.

Nonnie spelled out Galadriel as patiently as Gilly might have spelled out a hard word for W.E. 'Her school records will be sent directly to you. She's been in school in Maryland.'

'Maryland?' The same tone of voice used earlier for Hopkins.

It was a scene that was to repeat itself with variations many times in those first couple of weeks. 'Hopkins?' they always asked. 'Galadriel? How do you spell that?' 'Maryland, did you say?'

Gilly had had plenty of practice staring down sneers, but it was hard to imagine that someone like Nonnie had. But Nonnie looked straight down her short nose at every sneer and they stopped, at least the face-to-face ones did. Nonnie was gutsier than she looked.

But everything would be all right for them both now. Courtney was coming.

'It's silly to be nervous, isn't it?' Nonnie said. 'She's my own daughter. It's just that it's been so long. And she was hardly speaking to her father and me in those days. What will we say to each other?'

Oh, Nonnie. If I knew what mothers and daughters said to each other, wouldn't I tell you? How should I know?

'She'll think I've gotten terribly old. My hair was quite dark when she left.'

'Yeah?' She tried to put Courtney's hair on Nonnie's head. It didn't work.

'Would you think it was very silly of me to get a rinse?'

'A rinse?'

'Just to cover a little of the grey?'

Nonnie a Clairol girl? 'Why not?'

'Let's do it!' So while Nonnie was rinsed and curled, Gilly was cut and blown.

'You look lovely, my dear.'

Nonnie looked totally unnatural, but then Gilly had never seen her with black hair before. Maybe she'd look great to Courtney. 'You look nice, too,' she lied.

Money, though not as scarce as at Trotter's, was hardly in the supply hinted at in the letters to W.E. Nevertheless, Nonnie seemed determined to prepare royally for Courtney's return. They bought a Christmas tree that would touch the high ceiling of the living room and had to hire a neighbour's boy to carry it from the back of the old station wagon into the house and help them set it up.

Every ornament they hung had a family history, and Gilly half listened as Nonnie recounted each tale. She was too excited to concentrate fully, but she did grasp that the lopsided pasteboard star was one that Chadwell had made in the third grade. Most of the glued-on glitter had long departed. There was a yarn snowman that Courtney had made when a Brownie; it was grey now, and beginning to ravel. And there were yards of tattered paper chains. 'You sure you want to put these chains on?' Gilly asked Nonnie.

'Oh, we have to have the chains. We always had the chains.'

So Gilly glued the chains together as best she could and hung them. The whole effect was appalling – a pile of junk. But then she put on three boxes of tinsel, one strand at a time, so that the entire tree was under a silver veil. In a dark room with only the Christmas tree lighted, it wasn't bad. Not a department-store display, but not bad.

Nonnie slipped her glasses on and off her nose, trying to take in the sight, and finally let them hang on the ribbon around her neck while she clapped her hands like a little girl. 'I can't remember ever before having such a lovely tree,' she said.

Neither, after she thought about it, could Gilly.

December 20

Dear Gilly,

So your Mom is coming to see you? You must be real excited. Mr Randolph, William Ernest, and me wishes you lots of luck.

By the way, William Ernest come home yesterday with a bloody nose. You know me, I like to die, but he was prouder than a punch-drunk pickle. Mr Evans call me up to complain about my kid fighting at school but took to laughing too hard to finish. What do you think about that?

Sincerely, your friend,
Maime M. Trotter

*Pow!* That's what she thought of that.

# Homecoming

The plane was late. It seemed to Gilly that everything in this world that you can't stand to wait one extra minute for is always late. Her stomach was pretzeled with eagerness and anxiety. She stood sweating in the chill of the huge waiting room, the perspiration pouring down the sleeves of her new blouse. She'd probably ruin it and stink besides.

Then, suddenly, when she'd almost stopped straining her eyes with looking at it, the door opened, and people began to come off the motor lounge into the airport. All kinds of people, all sizes, all colours, all of them rushing. Many looking about for family or friends, finding them with little cries of joy and hugs. Tired fussy babies, children dragging on their mothers. Businessmen, heads down, swinging neat thin leather briefcases. Grandparents laden with shopping bags of Christmas presents. But no Courtney.

The pretzel turned to stone. It was all a lie. She would never come. The door blurred. Gilly wanted to leave. She didn't want to cry in the stupid airport, but just at that moment she heard Nonnie say in a quavering voice, 'Courtney.'

'Hello, Nonnie.'

But this person wasn't Courtney. It couldn't be Courtney! Courtney was tall and willowy and gorgeous. The woman who stood before them was no taller than Nonnie and just as plump, although she wore a long cape, so it was hard to make out her real shape. Her hair was long, but it was dull and stringy – a dark version of Agnes Stokes's, which had always needed washing. A flower child gone to seed. Gilly immediately pushed aside the disloyal thought.

Nonnie had sort of put her hand on the younger woman's arm in a timid embrace, but there was a huge embroidered shoulder bag between the two of them. 'This is Galadriel, Courtney.'

For a second, the smile, the one engraved on Gilly's soul, flashed out. The teeth were perfect. She was face to face with Courtney Rutherford Hopkins. She could no longer doubt it. 'Hi.' The word almost didn't come out. She wondered what she was supposed to do. Should she try to kiss Courtney or something?

At this point Courtney hugged her, pressing the huge bag into Gilly's chest and stomach and saying across her shoulder to Nonnie, 'She's as tall as I am,' sounding a little as though Gilly weren't there.

'She's a lovely girl,' said Nonnie.

'Well, of course, she is,' Courtney stepped back and smiled her gorgeous heart-shattering smile. 'She's mine, isn't she?'

Nonnie smiled back, rather more weakly than her daughter had. 'Maybe we should get your luggage.'

'I've got it,' said Courtney, slapping her shoulder bag. 'It's all right here.'

Nonnie looked a little as though she'd been smacked in the face. 'But –' she began and stopped.

'How many clothes can you wear in two days?'

Two days? Then Courtney had come to get her after all.

'I told you on the phone that I'd come for Christmas and see for myself how the kid was doing...'

'But when I sent you the money...'

Courtney's face was hard and set with lines between the

brows. 'Look. I came, didn't I? Don't start pushing me before I'm hardly off the plane. My god, I've been gone thirteen years, and you still think you can tell me what to do.' She slung the bag behind her back. 'Let's get out of here.'

Nonnie shot Gilly a look of pain. 'Courtney –'

She hadn't come because she wanted to. She'd come because Nonnie had paid her to. And she wasn't going to stay. And she wasn't going to take Gilly back with her. 'I will always love you.' It was a lie. Gilly had thrown away her whole life for a stinking lie.

'I gotta go to the bathroom,' Gilly said to Nonnie. She prayed they wouldn't follow her there, because the first thing she was going to do was vomit, and the second was run away.

She tried to vomit, but nothing happened. She was still shaking from the effort when she dropped her coins in the pay telephone beside the restroom and dialled. It rang four times.

'Hello.'

'Trotter, it's me, Gilly.' God, don't let me break down like a baby.

'Gilly, honey. Where are you?'

'Nowhere. It doesn't matter. I'm coming home.'

She could hear Trotter's heavy breathing at the other end of the line. 'What's the matter, baby? Your mom didn't show?'

'No, she came.'

'Oh, my poor baby.'

Gilly was crying now. She couldn't help herself. 'Trotter, it's all wrong. Nothing turned out the way it's supposed to.'

'How you mean supposed to? Life ain't supposed to be nothing, 'cept maybe tough.'

'But I always thought that when my mother came...'

'My sweet baby, ain't no one ever told you yet? I reckon I thought you had that all figured out.'

'What?'

'That all that stuff about happy endings is lies. The only ending in this world is death. Now that might or might not be happy, but either way, you ain't ready to die, are you?'

'Trotter, I'm not talking about dying. I'm talking about coming home.'

But Trotter seemed to ignore her. 'Sometimes in this world things come easy, and you tend to lean back and say, "Well, finally, happy ending. This is the way things is supposed to be." Like life owed you good things.'

'Trotter –'

'And there is lots of good things, baby. Like you coming to be with us here this fall. That was a mighty good thing for me and William Ernest. But you just fool yourself if you expect good things all the time. They ain't what's regular – don't nobody owe 'em to you.'

'If life is so bad, how come you're so happy?'

'Did I say bad? I said it was tough. Nothing to make you happy like doing good on a tough job, now is there?'

'Trotter, stop preaching at me. I want to come home.'

'You're home, baby. Your grandma is home.'

'I want to be with you and William Ernest and Mr Randolph.'

'And leave her all alone? Could you do that?'

'Dammit, Trotter. Don't try to make a stinking Christian out of me.'

'I wouldn't try to make nothing out of you.' There was a quiet at the other end of the line. 'Me and William Ernest and Mr Randolph kinda like you the way you are.'

'Go to hell, Trotter,' Gilly said softly.

A sigh. 'Well, I don't know about that. I had planned on settling permanently somewheres else.'

'Trotter' – She couldn't push the word hard enough to keep the squeak out – 'I love you.'

'I know, baby. I love you, too.'

She put the phone gently on the hook and went back into the bathroom. There she blew her nose on toilet tissue and washed her face.

By the time she got back to an impatient Courtney and a stricken Nonnie, she had herself well under control.

'Sorry to make you wait,' Gilly said. 'I'm ready to go home now.' No clouds of glory, perhaps, but Trotter would be proud.

## Watch All Night

*John Foster*

Tess is an only child, quiet and introspective. After a bout of anaemia, she is allowed to go to London for a few days to see her father, a nuclear scientist who works in an Arab state governed by a military dictatorship. She is enjoying her trip until a number of frightening things happen. Her father disappears, then the hotel staff claim that she checked in alone, and when Ingrid the chambermaid also disappears, Tess is left to unravel the mystery and try to prove she is not going mad. A gripping novel, filmed by Granada Television.

## Cunningham's Little Red Record Book

*Bronnie Cunningham*

Stuffed full of all sorts of incredible facts, this mine of essential – and, if the truth be told, non-essential – information has all the answers. Your imagination will be stretched and your brain truly boggled as you read of the incredible coincidences and amazing events that flourish in the world, put together by the compiler of *The Puffin Joke Book* and *Funny Business*.

## Heard about the Puffin Club?

... it's a way of finding out more about Puffin books
and authors, of winning prizes (in competitions),
sharing jokes, a secret code, and perhaps seeing your
name in print! When you join you get a copy
of our magazine, *Puffin Post*, sent to you four times
a year, a badge and a membership book.

For details of subscription and an application form,
send a stamped addressed envelope to:

> *The Puffin Club Dept A*
> *Penguin Books Limited*
> *Bath Road*
> *Harmondsworth*
> *Middlesex UB7 0DA*

and if you live in Australia, please write to:

> *The Australian Puffin Club*
> *Penguin Books Australia Limited*
> *P.O. Box 257*
> *Ringwood*
> *Victoria 3134*